This Heart's

M000195351

Wives Wanted: For the cowboys of Mule Hollow!

Bound for California, candy-maker Dottie Hart can't turn her back on a teenage girl hitchhiking her way to Mule Hollow, Texas. Fearful for the girl, Dottie changes directions and heads toward the tiny town that's advertising for wives for its lonesome cowboys. Sheriff Brady Cannon has enough trouble on his hands with the chaos the matchmaking ladies in town have caused with their off the wall scheme to save the tiny town. When the gorgeous candy-maker with a heart as sweet a sugar shows up he's suddenly dreaming of candy kisses and forever...but he's got his own reasons for staying single.

Can the Texas Matchmakers...or "posse" as some are starting to call them, rope him into the herd of lonesome cowboys bound for love?

Clean and wholesome romance!

Note: This book was previously published as *No Place Like Home*. This edition includes some fun extras.

THIS HEART'S YOURS, COWBOY

Texas Matchmakers Series, Book Three
Enhanced Edition

DEBRA CLOPTON

CHAPTER ONE

Glancing at the lone figure standing in the reflection of her side mirror, Dottie Hart stomped hard on the brake and wrangled her prehistoric motor home to a groaning halt.

What in the world is that kid thinking?

In less than a shake and a wiggle Dottie was out the door watching the girl jog toward her along the shoulder of the hectic highway. The world was full of crazed people just waiting for the opportunity to snatch up a girl like that...and here she was hitchhiking!

Well, it wasn't happening today, because Dottie's new prayer each morning was for the Lord to use her any way He chose. Looked like today He'd put this girl in her pathway.

"Hey, thanks for stopping," the girl said, dropping

her bag with a thud at Dottie's feet.

She looked to be in her late teens, maybe even twenty, older than Dottie had first thought, but still too young to be hitchhiking...no one was old enough to do that!

"Don't thank me. Thank the Lord," Dottie said. "He's the one watching your back today." *Thank You, Father. Thank you so much for putting me in her pathway.*

The teen lifted her chin defiantly, eyebrows knitted together. "Oh, brother! You aren't one of those wacko people who go around picking up hitchhikers just so you can cram that religion stuff down their throats, are you?"

Dottie shook her head. "Do I look that brave? I just thought I'd mention why I decided to give you a lift." The girl relaxed a bit but still looked wary. "Okay, I'll accept the lift 'cause I need it. Just don't get carried away with the God stuff. Me and the big guy aren't getting along so well right now."

Dottie studied the teen. "That's too bad. Here, let me help you carry that thing."

"Hey, hey!" The girl jerked her bag away when Dottie reached for it. "I carry my own bags, lady. You may have wheels but I've got backbone. And I gotta tell you, by the look of your wheels, my backbone's looking

2

like it's the winner. How old is this thing anyway?"

"Hey! Watch what you say about my rig!" Dottie patted the side of her RV. "It's ugly, sure, but this baby's gonna get us where we need to go long before it wheezes its last breath." Walking to the cabin door, she opened it then glanced over her shoulder. "If you're still up for a ride, chuck that bag inside and let's hit the road."

Climbing back into her faithful RV, Dottie tried to calm the jitters threatening to set in. Tried to reassure herself that it was going to be fine.

You've really picked up a hitchhiker!

True, but calm down, she told herself. There were no hoodlums hiding in the bushes, using the girl as a front. She didn't appear to be a teenage ax murderer, so everything was going to be okay. Really.

A woman had to take a risk every once in a while, didn't she? On the other hand, if she truly believed God put people in a person's life for a reason, then this was no accident—and she did believe that with all her heart. God had given her a second chance at life and she'd made a promise that she was bound and determined to follow through with it. This was a test.

Not that she was an advocate for a woman traveling alone to pick up strangers off the side of the road. She'd never done anything like this before. And when her brother learned what she'd done he might skin her alive, but it felt right. And that was good enough for Dottie.

For goodness' sake, she was about to start working at a women's shelter—a home for women at risk. How could she live with herself if she passed one on the side of the road and didn't help her!

She couldn't. And that was that. Decision made— case closed. So relax.

Grabbing the big plastic bag of Gummi Bunnies off the dashboard, she held it out. "Want a handful?"

"Sure," the girl said, slamming the passenger's door closed and reaching for the bag.

Watching her dig into the candy, Dottie relaxed even further. True, she was supposed to be back in California as quickly as possible, time was of the essence, but this girl had obviously needed a friend.

"There's drinks in the fridge if you need something. And real food." Biting back any other reservations, she smiled. "I'm Dottie Hart," she offered, meeting the girl's hazel eyes that were similar to her own.

"I'm Cassie Bates," she said, nibbling a mouthful of the chewy little bunnies from her open palm. "I'm on my way to Mule Hollow—where the men grow tall and the women aren't at all."

"Do what?" Dottie laughed, digging out a handful of candy for herself. "What's that supposed to mean?"

Cassie gaped at her. "You know, *love is in the hair and the air!*" She sang the line.

All the while Dottie stared. Okay—so maybe something *was* loose and it wasn't Dottie's screws.

"You really don't know what I'm talking about?"

The silent "Duh!" at the end of Cassie's question hung in the air between them.

"Not a clue." But she was curious. Extremely curious.

Cassie dug in her back pocket and pulled out a bundle of newspaper clippings and waved them. Neatly cut and folded in a half-inch-thick bundle, the clippings were very organized.

"This is Mule Hollow, Texas. The tiny town way out here in the middle of nowhere that advertised for women who want to get married, move there and live happily ever after."

Oh, brother. Dottie had heard it all now. "You're saying they, this town, is advertising for women to come marry the local men."

"Yes. Are you deaf? It's all right here in Molly Popp's column." She waved the clippings.

"Who is Molly Popp?"

"Molly Popp?" Another duh. "She writes this really cool article every week about what's happening in Mule Hollow. *Everybody's* following the stories.

Where have you been? The moon?"

If she only knew, Dottie thought. "Let's just say I haven't had much time for reading. Who would think up something so outlandish? Are you sure it's a real story and not some promotional gimmick made up to hook readers?"

"Oh, it's real. And I'm going there to change my life."

Now, *that* was something Dottie could connect with. "And how are you going to do that?"

"I'm going to find me a husband."

"You can't just go into a town and pick a husband out like he was a shirt waiting to be bought off the rack."

"Says who? You should read these articles." Another wave of newspaper clippings. "These are nice guys. Guys who know how to treat a woman and want to get married. And stay married."

Dottie could *not* believe her ears. But obviously Cassie was determined to do this, this…harebrained thing, so what exactly did that mean? She took a breath.

Okay, Lord, what's the plan?

She knew the answer before she asked the question. She'd committed to the task the minute she pulled onto the shoulder, actually the minute she prayed that morning for the Lord to use her today. Her granddad always said, never ask the Lord to put someone in your path unless you mean business. The good Lord would take you up on the offer every time…

But taking a detour? Going to some really weird little town out in the middle of nowhere—a town that *advertised* for wives! Now, that just wasn't a blip on her screen of possible scenarios.

However, even being alive, sitting here being allowed the opportunity to even consider such a scenario was a gift…

She'd missed three months of her life lying in a hospital bed on the verge of death. Three months. She closed her eyes, willed away the panic that still sought to overpower her just thinking about the dark hours that led up to her stay in that hospital bed—as always thoughts of that time practically caused her to hyperventilate. She willed away the visible signs of her ordeal, calling on the Lord, as always, for help. This was no time to scare her passenger.

It was true, she had much to overcome. But she had more to celebrate. God had saved her! He'd performed nothing less than a miracle in keeping her alive through the hurricane that had devastated her home and tried to destroy her life. After a person spent almost three days trapped in a dark hole crushed beneath her home, her life seeping away with every moment that passed, there was nothing less she could do than try and repay God's faithfulness.

The payment for that debt waited for her in California. She was needed there in a desperate way—Cassie Bates, with her weird agenda, hadn't been in the equation. And yet, God had crossed their paths. Cassie needed a friend. Someone to watch over her, to get her to a safe place and to make certain that she was going to be all right.

How could Dottie pass her by? God had sent a special task force of heroes to dig her from the cold, wet depths of a lonely would-be grave. He'd put her in their path and now He'd put Cassie in her path. She had to accept the call.

It might still be California or bust, but she could take a little detour. Anticipation rippled through her.

God worked in mysterious ways…

"So," she said, drawing Cassie's bright gaze. "Exactly how do we get to this Mule Hollow?"

Sheriff Brady Cannon stood inside Pete's Feed and Seed looking out the window at Mule Hollow's deserted street and the late-afternoon shadows creeping across the blacktop. The bedraggled motor home that turned the corner onto Main Street almost caused him to choke on a sunflower seed.

The thing was about twenty years old, its front grille warped, giving an impression of a crooked grin as it carried its cargo. Cargo was tied down at precariously odd angles on top of the comical-looking thing. There was white wicker furniture and other stuff he couldn't quite make out bulging from the roof in wild disarray. A mental picture of a cartoon character moving cross-country sprang to mind.

Watching the funny-looking RV amble along he was a little surprised to see a vendor this early. The first annual Mule Hollow Trade Days event didn't start for four days yet. Which meant his headaches wouldn't start for four short days either, days he wasn't taking for granted. Early birds weren't exactly his idea of a good thing.

When the pitiful RV suddenly wheezed and smoke erupted from under the hood, it was as if the animation had come to life! "Oh boy, let the games begin," he groaned.

Reacting on instinct, he tossed his handful of sunflower seeds into the garbage, grabbed Pete's fire extinguisher from beside the counter and hit the door at a run.

Black smoke billowed from beneath the hood as he concentrated on the hot latch, coughing from the fumes as they engulfed him. When the latch finally gave and he lifted the reluctant hood, he was forced to jump back to avoid the shooting flames filling the compartment. Thankfully, Pete's extinguisher was primed and ready and he had the fire out within seconds.

Not that it saved the motor—it was toast.

"Oh no!"

At the gasp, he spun around to find a thin woman with raven-black hair and pale hazel eyes. Stricken by the sight of the steaming engine she swayed—Brady dropped the extinguisher and grabbed her just as her legs buckled. He was struck by her lightness, again by her paleness as he swept her into his arms. By the way her delicate cheekbones were starkly pronounced by the thinness of her face. She didn't look exactly well. As he studied her, her eyes fluttered, she bit her lip and he could almost see sheer willpower forcing her eyelids to remain open.

"Dottie, are you okay?" a teenage girl exclaimed, concern written all over her impish face as she danced from foot to foot.

"Fine. I'm fine," she assured the girl.

Brady disagreed completely with her assessment of the situation. "Miss, you don't look so good. I think—"

"I'm fine. Really, you can put me down now."

The strength in her words and the determination

he could see in her eyes had him doing as he was instructed. "It's your call." Carefully he set her on her feet, glad when she didn't sway again. A bit of color crept into her cheeks, but she remained fairly pale, although he could see that there was a tinge of tan overlaying her paleness.

"I'm Dottie." She extended her delicate hand and smiled engagingly. "Dottie Hart. I'm sorry for my…well, for that." She rolled her eyes and waved her hand as if shooing the episode away.

Obviously Dottie Hart did not enjoy being fragile. She looked embarrassed by the show of weakness. "Nothing to be sorry about," he said. "But I hate to tell you that your motor doesn't look good." Her lips flattened into a straight line. "By the way, I'm Brady Cannon."

Her gaze shifted from the RV to him. "Sheriff Cannon," she said, her gaze dropping to the badge pinned to his white shirt.

Her voice was smooth, with an edge of softness to it. And her eyes… "Actually, everyone calls me Brady."

She nodded but didn't smile. Her gaze swept back to the engine. "Thank you for putting out the fire. Is there a mechanic in Mule Hollow who could get me moving again?"

She looked back at him with her question. Two

vertical lines formed between her eyebrows. He could almost see her mind turning as she concentrated on her problem.

"We have a mechanic, but I hate to tell you that he's out of town at the moment. He had a family emergency that needed tending to. But he's due back next week. A mechanic might not be able to fix your engine, though."

"Well." She compressed her lips, glanced toward the young girl, then met his eyes straight on. "We'll see."

She took a deep breath, visibly making a decision. "I planned to stay a few days anyway."

"That's what I thought. Looks like you're the first one here. We can go ahead and get you all set up, and then Prudy can come by and check the motor over at the site when he gets back to town on Monday. I'll get a few of the boys to help me with your rig and we'll get it to a spot—"

"Hey, Dottie, here it is," the teen yelled, interrupting him. She was waving excitedly from across the street where she'd trotted while they were talking.

Dottie smiled, turning slightly toward the girl. Brady's gaze snagged on her smile, captivated by it and the measureless depth of her gaze. There was something about the way she watched things.

"Just look at it, Dottie," Cassie exclaimed. "What," Dottie laughed, and even in the dying light her eyes twinkled like sunlight reflecting off cool water.

Brady knew the *it* was the hot-pink salon the kid was standing in front of.

"It's Lacy Brown's Heavenly Inspirations," she called. "It's just like in the articles."

She plastered her face to the glass and peered into the window like a two-year-old. It was a now-familiar sight to Brady and the other Mule Hollow residents. Over the last few months when women came to town after hours and Lacy had gone home for the night, there was much peering through the glass. The ads had started it, but Molly's articles about Lacy and Mule Hollow had garnered widespread fame. It was bafflement to him and most days a headache.

"She really loves this place." Dottie turned to him.

"Mule Hollow and Lacy's place seem to have that effect on some people. The residents are banking on it. Just wait until this weekend when everyone starts getting here. There'll be more smears on that window than just Cassie's."

"I noticed you said I was the first. It sounds like you're expecting a lot of people this weekend?"

Brady chuckled and stuck a hand in his back pocket. "You could say that. I've become a believer, and when the ladies say there will be a crowd, I trust that they know what they're talking about. Hang on—I'll get somebody out here to help get you off the road and set up. We weren't expecting anybody until the day after tomorrow, but this'll work. You just sit tight and I'll be right back."

Dottie watched the good sheriff stride away. She'd nearly passed out! She hated when that happened. And in front of the sheriff—the totally breathtaking, giant of a man—

"Where's the sheriff going?" Cassie asked, jogging up beside her. Her energy reminded Dottie of her own before the accident. Oh, how she missed the health she'd so taken for granted. Watching Cassie, she was all the more determined to regain every bit of herself that she'd had before the accident. She was twenty-eight years old and used to love jogging every day. She just needed to be patient and keep up her workouts and she'd grow strong again.

"Yoo-hoo, anybody in there?" Cassie waved her hand in front of Dottie's eyes, jolting her back to the present.

"Sorry," she said. "He went to get help to move us off the street."

Cassie spun around and stared after Brady. "Do you think he's going to get some hunky cowboys? That'd be great. Really great."

Looking at the open adulation beaming from Cassie's eyes, Dottie felt it was probably best to try and rein her in a bit.

"Cassie, maybe it would be good if you didn't throw yourself at these guys."

Her eyes widened. "Who's throwing themselves? Anyway, a girl's gotta do what a girl's gotta do. Right? Wow! Would ya look at that!"

A huge black truck was lumbering around the corner, efficiently cutting off Dottie's thoughts. The thing was, like, five feet off the ground with bumpers the size of a cattle guard and big ol' lights sticking up on top of the cab like bulging frog eyes. My oh my— *it's a monster!* Wow…she was as pole axed by it as Cassie.

And that was saying something, because Cassie went speechless gaping at the thing.

When the driver hopped to the ground Cassie took a step back and studied at the young man. He was dressed in rumpled jeans, boots and a weathered T-shirt. He'd hopped from behind the steering wheel looking like a guy ready to take on any adventure that came his way. He looked like he was ready to have a good time.

Then Sheriff Brady stepped down from the passenger's seat, looking every bit the man ready to take charge of this little misadventure. Dottie had to fight her own impulse to step back and gasp. The man was breathtaking. It was enough to make a girl on a mission that was far, far away from Mule Hollow sick to her fluttering stomach. *Get a grip, girl.*

She shook herself mentally at her ridiculous reaction and focused on the younger man. *Ignore the sheriff.* She didn't need the distraction.

The cowboy tipped his hat at her and then at Cassie, at whom he also flashed a one-hundred-watt, crooked smile. "Looks like y'all could use a hand. Give me a sec and I'll have you ladies set up."

He began pulling chains from the bed of his truck and then practically dived beneath the front of Dottie's motor home. Not before she saw him sneak another look at Cassie, who was catching flies with her open mouth.

The sheriff sauntered over and stood next to Dottie and she had to fight the urge to walk away. She wasn't a rude person and it bothered her, this odd rankling of her nerves. "He knows what he's doing, doesn't he?" she asked, dismayed that it sounded as if she was questioning his good sense.

"Jake can pull anything out of anywhere."

"How does he know how to do that?" The moment the question was out she wanted it back. Why, the sheriff looked at her like she'd lost her mind!

"He's not much more than a kid," he said in an even tone, hiding laughter. He might have tried to hide it but she could see it. His lips were positively quivering. *And* his eyes had crinkled at the edges.

"And don't you see the *size* of the wheels on that truck," he continued. "Jake and his friends spend the better part of every other night mudding across half this county. Believe me when I say he can pull anything."

Well, yes, she could see all of that. But still—"That should do it." Jake scooted from beneath her vehicle, sprang to his feet and walked jauntily over and attached the chain to the ball of his truck. Dottie heard an audible sigh from Cassie as he hurried to the RV's open door, leaned in and adjusted the gearshift. By the time he slammed the door and jogged back toward them, Dottie had forgotten her trepidations and was on board with the whole "he can pull anything" campaign. He certainly seemed competent.

"Can I give you a lift over to the site?" he asked.

"Yeah! I mean, sure!" Cassie gushed.

Miss Tough Girl had turned into a breathless shambles. Dottie nearly fell over when the girl practically skipped to the huge truck and hoisted herself up into the high seat!

And then, just like that, Dottie found herself alone with Sheriff Brady. Not at *all* a situation she was comfortable with.

"Shall we?" he drawled, sweeping his hand to follow the truck.

Dottie hesitated in the dying light, then fell into step beside him.

Dark was nearly upon them as they walked down the road together. Through the shadows she stole a glance at the handsome man. He overpowered everything around him…including her good sense. He made her aware of every step they took. And she didn't like it. Not one bit!

Out of nowhere her heart trembled and sparked. *No!*

She almost tripped in her surprise—

"Are you okay?" he asked, cupping her elbow to steady her.

"F-fine," she stuttered, pulling away. This was not good. She was here in this adorable town because of Cassie. *Cassie* was the one window-shopping for a man. As for her, Dottie Marie "Fickle" Hart, her life was complicated.

She gave the sheriff her best nonchalant glance. It didn't matter how good-looking a man he was, or how crazy her pulse was jigging at his nearness. It didn't matter how kind he appeared to be. And it truly, certainly didn't matter if he made her feel as weak on the inside as her body felt on the outside.

Sheriff Brady Cannon seemed like a great guy, who had no wedding ring on his finger. But none of these facts mattered. And that was the way it would remain. She had an agenda that left no room for infatuations of the personal kind.

Period. She wasn't that fickle.

She had an agenda of the heavenly sort, a payback for a life changed. And that thought was all it took to get her head on straight again.

Too late, Brady realized he hadn't been thinking straight when he'd suggested they walk. Dottie seemed a little unsteady. She was obviously weak, a woman didn't pass out without a reason. What a buffoon he was! And now here they were, walking along and she was limping—stumbling even, and trying hard to hide it. He slowed his pace to match hers, causing her to glance at him, her eyes wide.

"I needed the exercise," she blurted out as if reading his mind, as if not wanting to admit a weakness. Her words were breathless. "I, well...I get a little stove up when I ride long distances all at once."

He nodded, noticing how she moved away from him.

"You came far?" He glanced at her, curious about her but trying not to be intrusive, a hard thing for a cop.

She nodded but didn't look at him. "Yes."

Single-word answers were not what he was looking for. Though his beat was different here in his tiny hometown, his previous life as a cop on the streets of Houston still imprinted everything he did. He wanted details and suddenly he was full of questions. "How far? Where are you from?" *Smooth, Brady.*

"I started out in Florida five days ago."

"Ouch! That is a long way."

"Oh, yes, but most people would've made it here in three days. I hurt my hip in an accident and can only travel so far before I'm forced to stop for the day. That is *if* I want to be able to move the next day."

"What kind of accident?" *What are you doing, Brady?*

She locked her arms and looked into the distance, as if she really didn't want to elaborate, then focused back on him. "I was bullheaded enough to think I could protect my home from a hurricane."

"Ohhh."

She grimaced. "Sounds stupid, I know, believe me, and the house collapsed on me, despite my personal efforts at holding it up under Category 3 winds."

He could tell, though she gave a quick smile, there

was nothing funny about her ordeal. However, he knew only too well in his line of work that sometimes humor took the edge off.

"I spent three months in the hospital. I was a mess. Not a vacation I'd recommend at all, as you can imagine. I spent several months rehabilitating. I'm doing great, considering everything. I can't run a marathon yet, though."

She met his gaze, her expression blank and unreadable but entirely captivating with the intensity of her words. How much pain and suffering must she have endured? It was obvious Dottie still hurt. He could see it. As a cop he'd learned to read people pretty well. And Dottie was a book that had to be read slowly. Carefully.

"But I will." She smiled.

He stopped. They'd made the fifty-yard walk to the corner. Though she hadn't voiced any of it, he had a vivid picture of this fragile woman in pain unlike any he'd ever experienced. Looking into her eyes, he searched harder this time. He glimpsed a shadow of... anger, despite the smile. He'd seen it before...but suddenly he wondered if she even knew it was there. "I bet you will," he said. "You impress me as a person who can do anything she sets her mind to."

To his surprise she shook her head, and her eyes

misted with tears.

"Only by the grace of God." She lifted her chin and blinked away the mist. "You can't imagine how many times I felt like quitting. But that verse! It kept popping into my head, forcing me on, reminding me that God was there, right beside me. The truth is—until I was so low I couldn't get any lower, I never really understood that I can really do all things through Christ, who strengthens me." Her earnest expression melted into another smile. "That's what got me through grueling rehab, through days that I couldn't take on my own. God's faithful. He can take the worst of times and make something good. If we let Him."

Brady was in trouble.

He knew it the moment she smiled at him again.

He knew the moment she lifted her eyes to the sky and winked, like she and God had a secret. It was as if she was defying the tears and the anger to grasp the joy. Oh yeah, Brady was in trouble all right, because although he'd only known Dottie Hart for less than thirty minutes, he knew he wanted in on her secret.

CHAPTER TWO

Mule Hollow was getting ready for a pretty big day. Even in the dusky light Dottie could see there were spots sectioned off in the field for booths and trailers. They'd even set up electrical services for vendors, which she wasn't. But how coincidental that she was both a baker and a candy maker on her way to California, who just happened to find Cassie on the side of the road, which brought her to Mule Hollow, where her motor home happened to die. She smiled, reminded of the song about the old woman who swallowed the fly. It had dawned on her just now talking to Sheriff Brady—Mule Hollow seemed like a safe place to be stranded. God had protected her. Even before she knew she needed protecting. *How sweet was that?*

He'd even given her a way of saving her money for California. At least most of it. Instead of dipping into her bank account she now had a way to pay for the repairs to her RV...she could make and sell some simple candy and baked goods over the weekend and have a little extra money to help pay the mechanic. She wouldn't have to tap into her insurance.

Everything was fine, except for the time factor. But that was what had her winking toward heaven a moment ago. She was on God's time schedule, so she was going to try and relax. Try not to worry. Really...why should she? She'd prayed for a safe trip to California— never had she envisioned God would take her a hundred miles out of her way to get her there safely. But the reality was that if she'd been on the highway when the engine burst into flames—she hated to think about it. For one, she may not have been able to stop the fire; two, she'd have become a hitchhiker herself.

And three, she might have lost everything. Again.

Not that much meant anything to her anyway. When a person lay dying beneath all her worldly stuff, stuff accumulated over a lifetime, it changed a person's perspective. But she had to admit that her RV mattered to her. It had belonged to her granddad and there was a host of memories inside the poor-looking thing.

Besides, it had been beat up and banged up during the same storm that beat her up...she and her prehistoric monstrosity were survivors.

Sheriff Brady pushed his hat back a bit and looked down at her, and she realized with a start that he'd said something. He probably thought she was crazy since not everyone winked at heaven and grinned like a goofball.

"I'm sorry, what did you say?" she asked, focusing on him.

"I said, the rest of the vendors will start trickling in tomorrow afternoon, but the actual event won't start until Friday." He paused, touching her shoulder with his finger, halting her. "Are you okay?"

His touch was gentle and Dottie tried to ignore the warmth that seemed to radiate from it. "Yes, I get kinda weird sometimes, thinking about how good God is, that's all."

He smiled. "I have to say I've never seen anyone wink at God."

"Get outta here." Dottie shoved his arm. "You're telling me you never winked at God."

He laughed. "I'd have to say that'd be an affirmative. But it was cute."

She laughed and their gazes locked.

The laugh died in her throat. His face was shadowed, his eyes shimmered, in the disappearing light. Suddenly it felt like a pebble dance across her stomach, instantly sending ripples radiating through her solar plexus. *Oh my!*

"L-look," she managed to say. "I have to explain something."

"What's that?" He dropped his chin and raised an eyebrow.

What in the world was happening to her? She was tired—it had been a long, a very long, hard day. "I didn't come here to be a vendor in the trade show."

She rattled out the words so fast that he stepped back, head cocked back a notch.

"You didn't?" He looked over his shoulder at the motor home being set up in the vending spot. The motor home that looked exactly like it wasn't out of place in a setting like this.

"Actually…" She snapped the words out. Ignoring—well, trying to focus on what had brought her here in the first place. "I picked Cassie up on the road. She was hitchhiking about a hundred miles away. I just couldn't stand seeing that young girl out there on the road, so I broke my 'no hitchhiker' rule." She made quotation marks in the air with her fingers. "I picked her up. When she started telling me where she was going I couldn't just drop her off somewhere along the way and hope someone else brought her safely here— I had to bring her."

Brady removed his Stetson and scrubbed his hand through his short brown hair.

And Dottie, drat her fickle brain, forgot everything for a moment. The man was gorgeous—even with the hat crease running across his forehead.

"You're telling me you went a *hundred* miles out of your way to bring a hitchhiker to Mule Hollow?"

She nodded, hearing the disbelief edging his words, understanding it completely. It was her reaction to him that she didn't have a clue about! "Not any hitchhiker. *Cassie.* Oh, wait—is hitchhiking against the law?"

The corners of Brady's lips curved engagingly and her stomach did a double back flip!

"Nope. Least not the last time I checked. Though it could possibly be bad for your health."

"Funny." She scrunched her face at him before she could stop herself. "I didn't want to get Cassie in trouble," she continued, regaining some composure. "I can't help feeling like I need to watch out for her. She knows everything about this town and has talked nonstop all the way here about finding herself a husband. It's like she's obsessed with getting a husband and getting him *yesterday.*"

"She wouldn't be the first woman looking for a husband—hold on just a minute. How old is she?"

"Bingo! I honestly don't know. I thought she was really young, too, but I don't think she's as young as I first believed. She wouldn't tell me earlier when I asked, claiming a lady doesn't tell her age."

He was instantly all law enforcement. A gleam lit his eyes and she could very nearly see his brain rolling. "I think I need to do some checking on Cassie. She could be in some kind of trouble."

"Please do, and thank you. Only, I don't want to scare her. I don't think it would be a good idea to let her know you're checking into her background. Is that possible? If she's a runaway she might get scared and run again if she's spooked."

"I agree," he answered. "It's a good thing you're going to be around for a while to keep an eye on her." Dottie couldn't agree more. She'd have to talk to her brother, Todd, let him know what was going on. Once he heard all the facts, he'd agree that looking out for Cassie was important. There wasn't too much she could do at the moment anyway in California, at least nothing until they heard whether they were going to keep the lease…she said a quick prayer that God would step in and save No Place Like Home. It was inconceivable to think that a place that was doing such wonderful work would have so many sudden problems. She forced away the worry, certain everything would be okay. God was taking care of her, surely He would take care of the women's shelter.

"Did you ever in your entire life see such a dreamy guy?" Cassie paused, filling her glass with water, and sighed.

Plumping her houseguest's pillow, Dottie tossed it up onto the bed above the RV's driving compartment, then picked up another one. Cassie had been beaming ever since Jake had driven up to help them. Dottie fully expected to see the girl float to her bunk at any moment.

A far cry from the hard-edged kid she'd picked up on the highway.

Dottie paused, mid-plump. "He's a dreamboat. But, Cassie, he can't be much more than twenty." It was a weak argument but all she had to try and slow Cassie down.

"And what's wrong with that?"

"Well, nothing. He just seemed...well, young." Dottie felt older than her twenty-eight years looking into Cassie's youthful face as she plopped into the table booth, and stared up at her, her chin in hand. Her bright gaze sent Dottie to check her cupboard. She really was uncomfortable giving advice, and she…well, she needed to see what supplies she had so she could start baking in the morning.

No, she needed to try and talk some sense into Cassie.

"How old are you, Dottie?"

"Hey, you're the girl who wouldn't tell me her age earlier this afternoon. Remember?"

"Well, that was before I knew you. Before I trusted you."

Trust.

Dottie's stomach soured thinking about how Brady was going to check on Cassie's background. Trust. "I'm twenty-eight. How old are you?"

"I'm really nineteen. Really. I know, I know, I don't look it. I hate people telling me I look younger. But if you look at me *really* close you can tell I'm not sixteen. Look, I have crow's-feet."

Dottie busted out laughing, turning toward her just in time to see Cassie pointing at the edges of her eyes. "Oh, brother!" True, she did look nineteen on second glance. Maybe. Once more she wondered about Cassie's background.

"Okay, you look nineteen, sort of. Don't you think that's a bit young to be so gung-ho about finding a husband right away? You do know that you need to fall in love."

"Hey, I *want* a husband and I'm gonna get one. I'll fall in love, but it's about…never mind. I'm too tired to think straight. What are you cooking tomorrow? Can I help?"

"Can you help?" Cassie had effectively changed the subject and Dottie let it slide. Tackling the subject of husband hunting with her was going to require alertness and at the moment she was worn out. "Aren't you the one who got me into this fix?"

Cassie chuckled. "That'd be me."

"Then, yes, you're about to learn to make candy. Tomorrow. We'll just make things like fudge and brownies though. Cooking in an RV is limiting. But we can make do. And the microwave can be utilized, too. Do you like to cook?"

Cassie's smile faded. "I—I can cook some. Your average can of beans and corn."

Something about the way she said that, despite her air of humor, made Dottie wonder if there was more to the story. There usually was.

"But—" she beamed "—I love fudge. It'll be cool learning how to make it. I wonder if Jake likes fudge. He said his boss told him to spend the next three days doing whatever Miss Norma told him to do, so he'll be around tomorrow."

"Who's that?"

"Norma Sue Jenkins. I can't wait to meet her and Adela and Esther Mae. They're the ladies who first put out the ad that brought Lacy Brown and Sheri Marsh to town. And then there's Molly, of course, and Sam. And Clint, and Cort and J.P. and Bob—"

"Whoa Nellie! How many people does this Molly write about?"

"Everyone...I think. I don't know though, 'cause she never wrote about Jake, and I'll tell you this—she should have. Although Bob's probably gonna be my man. Bob's special—"

"Bob? Who's Bob, and what do you mean 'your man'?" Dottie felt queasy.

"Bob Jacobs—he's been a headliner in Molly's stories. He's the main reason I came. He's the one I'm gonna marry."

Brady hopped from the cab of his tractor, his boots sending up a plume of dust from the barn floor as he landed. He needed a shower, a tall glass of iced tea and some unwinding time. Striding from the barn, he made his way across the expanse of Saint Augustine grass and flagstone separating the house and the barn. His mom and dad had outdone themselves when they'd built the huge two-story ranch house.

What a waste that he lived here alone.

He was still gnawing on that problem a short while later walking, freshly showered, from the silent house out onto the front porch. The sound of his bare footsteps echoed behind him, reminders that no single guy should have this much house all to himself.

Sinking to the top step, he relaxed against the porch post as he'd done a thousand times in his lifetime and took a sip of his tea. Besides being the sheriff, the only official emergency responder within twenty miles, he also ran his own cattle operation. It made for a very full plate. And that helped him not think so much about how the house was too big for him.

Or about how it would never hear the steps of children...

He inhaled sharply, feeling the warm breeze, smelling the dust and grass, laced with a faint sweetness from the ancient wisteria bush growing up the trellis. It was hard to believe he'd spent most of his youth planning his escape from the quiet of the country, Mule Hollow specifically.

And his parents' hopes and dreams for him.

His parents, had they lived to see his return, would have been happy...at least in theory. Dreams didn't always turn out the way they were dreamed, but he'd adapted to the reality of his return home.

Life was about illusions. And overcoming regrets. Dottie Hart.

The beautiful woman was special. The very essence of her being reached out and expressed the fact, he was certain, to everyone. He couldn't imagine she had this effect on him alone. It had to be momentary, though, she was just passing through. Here today, gone tomorrow—literally. So where were all these thoughts bombarding him coming from?

He took another drink of his iced tea, then studied a pebble on the porch step as he rubbed his big toe back and forth across it. He'd accepted when he'd come back to Mule Hollow that he was damaged goods and he hadn't really cared, yet the realization of his past and what it meant to his future had hit him full force today. For the first time in six years he suddenly cared that he was never going to marry and have a family.

It was ridiculous, he'd only just met Dottie and suddenly he was reevaluating his decisions.

He rose and walked to the end of the sidewalk, feeling the cool breeze on his sweat-dampened skin.

A picture of Dottie Hart formed in his mind. He couldn't believe she had gone that far out of her way to watch out for Cassie. He thought of the Good

Samaritan in the Bible. As a kid hearing that story in Sunday school, he hadn't thought what an unusual thing the man had done. If he had fallen off his bike and skinned his knee, there had always been a herd of people who would stop to help him.

But that had been a kid's perspective.

As a cop he'd seen firsthand just how unusual it was for someone to stop and help a person on the side of the road. People didn't want to get involved. People were afraid. With good reason.

He understood all too well how dangerous it was out there. Witnessed it up close and too personal. There was a part of him that wanted to tell Dottie what she'd done had been reckless, most especially for a woman alone in an area she didn't know. But his admiration for her overruled all his cautions. Again he wondered what her story was. He wondered... *Stop wondering, Brady.* Other than helping her figure out if Cassie Bates was a runaway, he didn't need to be wondering anything about Dottie.

Because the reality was, when each day ended, he would always walk into his house alone.

He'd chosen the life of a cop. He'd seen what happened to a cop's family when things went wrong in the line of duty. He'd thought watching his partner die in his arms was the hardest thing he'd ever done. But it had been watching Eddie's wife and two kids at the hospital that had changed his life.

He'd decided he would never put anyone he loved through that anguish.

Life was about choices. Good ones. Bad ones. Hard ones.

Turning, he strode to the hollow house, yanked open the screen door and stepped inside. Alone.

CHAPTER THREE

S am's Pharmaceuticals and Diner. Dottie read the sign splashed across the window. She smiled when she got close enough to read Eat at Your Own Peril, in small print. Sounded like Sam had a sense of humor.

When she awakened at her usual five in the morning she'd decided to check out the town and get a cup of coffee at the café. After working out and writing an e-mail to her brother, filling him in on what was happening, she'd made quick time coming over. She was excited to see the café Cassie had so vividly described to her with its jukebox that got stuck on forty-fives, playing the same song over and over again until it got good and ready to switch to something new.

Now, as she pushed open the door, she was instantly swept back in time. She felt like a child again, holding her granddad's hand as he bought her a soda pop at the general store just down the road from his house.

She loved those days.

Today the smells were of aged, oiled wood, bacon frying and the sweet scent of five-cent candy.... Inhaling deeply, she knew she could really love this place. The first person she saw when she stepped into the room was Sheriff Brady. Whether she wanted to admit it or not, the guy was the perfect adornment for any setting. All night she'd tried to tell herself there was no way he could be as handsome as she'd remembered.

Wrong.

He was everything she'd thought and more.

She had no time for this. She had an agenda to accomplish a long way from this small town. She was out of here in just a few days. So maybe she could look at the good sheriff, but that was it. No flirting, not that she was any good at flirting... The man was off-limits.

And you'd better remember it!

"Mornin', Miss Hart." His slow, easy drawl drew her to meet his eyes over his coffee cup as he took a sip of the steaming brew.

Dottie rubbed her suddenly clammy hands on the fronts of her workout pants and gave him a puny smile. She'd had a terrible night after she'd finally turned in, which was strange since she'd had such an interesting day. No way had she been expecting the nightmares to start again. When she'd awakened drenched in sweat, her heart pounding in the darkness, not even the small night-light she kept near her bed helped. The only relief, as always, had been to flee outside to the sweet open space where she could sit and talk to the Lord. Her caring Savior was always there for her.

Everything was fine now. "Good morning to you, Sheriff. Did you sleep well?"

He raised an eyebrow. "How about you?"

She shrugged, noticing the two eavesdropping older men sitting at the window hunched over a game of checkers that they were valiantly pretending to play. Instead, they were covertly listening.

She swallowed the cotton in her mouth. "New surroundings don't always lend themselves to a good night's rest. That and Cassie's snores. Whatever you do, don't tell her I said that. If there's one thing a young girl doesn't want getting out it's that she snores."

Brady chuckled. "You're probably right about that." Their gazes met. Dottie swallowed, forgetting everything for the moment as what felt like static electricity hummed between them. This was ridiculous! She'd hoped she'd only imagined the electricity. She hadn't imagined anything.

He cleared his throat, set his cup down and motioned

to the seat across from him. "Why don't you join me." She nodded, purely a reflex action. Besides, she did need to talk to him. Pushing away the butterflies tearing up her stomach, she crossed to his booth, glad her limp had eased up this morning. She slid into the bench across from him and looked him straight in the eye.

No childish infatuation was going to ambush her and muddle her good sense. She had a bigger agenda than this—this infatuation.

Oh, but he did have nice eyes.

In her peripheral vision the two checker players leaned out from their chairs a bit, getting their ears a little closer to the action. Shaking herself again, she smiled at them, even though they hadn't yet acknowledged her existence. Small towns always did have ears, and they had eyes, too, these two just hadn't caught on to the fact that she was on to them.

They were a good excuse not to look at Brady and she was thankful for the distraction.

"I saw you exercising earlier. When I pulled into town, I glanced down that way and you were getting after some crunches. It looked like a scene from the movie *G.I. Jane.*"

"It's part of my rehab." Mental and physical, but she didn't say that.

"At that rate you ought to be strong by tomorrow." She wished.

"That would be just fine with me. I never have been weak and I can't stand it. It makes me crazy."

In more ways than one—

Suddenly the swinging door to the back of the store flew open and a small wrinkled man burst through carrying a plate of bacon and eggs.

"How-do," he said as he plopped the plate down in front of the sheriff. "I heard what you said about being weak—you have a plate of this and you'll be as strong as an ox in two weeks' time. I promise."

Dottie laughed—but the little man wasn't laughing. He wasn't joking. *Oops.* The last thing she wanted was to hurt his feelings.

"Sam takes his breakfast serious," Sheriff Brady said, his eyes twinkling as he held back a chuckle of his own.

Sam crossed his wiry arms and locked eyes with her. "Eggs and bacon make a body strong. I don't care what these reports say nowadays. It's all that refined sugar that'll kill you. From the looks of ya, you ain't been eatin' much of anythang."

So much for thinking she was starting to get her figure back.

"Sam, this is Dottie Hart. She's the one I was

telling you about. Dottie, this is Sam. And those two over there are Applegate Thornton and Stanley Orr."

She recognized all the names from Cassie. "Glad to meet all of you gentlemen." The two checker players nodded and grunted something she couldn't quite make out. Sam held out his hand and she slipped hers into his and nearly fell out of the seat when he pumped it up and down so hard she felt as if it would come out of its socket. "My goodness, those eggs and bacon must work."

He beamed and dropped her hand, just in the nick of time.

"I'll have you a plate in a jiffy. Mean whilst, how 'bout some coffee?"

"Oh, yes, please."

Feeling a bit more relaxed, she watched him amble away.

"Is your arm okay?" Sheriff Brady asked, leaning across the table so that only she could hear the question.

"Yes, thanks. But boy, he's rather vigorous."

"Sam has a tendency to be violent when he shakes hands. I don't know why, but it's always the same." Dottie started to chuckle but bit it back as Sam reappeared with a cup of coffee. She thanked him and watched as he headed toward the kitchen with the promise that he'd be back in a few minutes.

She was about to say something more, when one of the checker players, Applegate, she thought it was, slapped his hand on the table and grunted loudly.

"Why'd you make that move?"

"'Cause I wanted to. It was the move to make, you old goat."

"I didn't see that checker there a minute ago."

"You sayin' I cheated?"

"I'm sayin' that that checker wasn't there a while ago."

"App, I ain't never had to beat you by cheatin', so why should I have to do it now?"

Not certain if she should be alarmed, or if this went on all the time, Dottie glanced from the two men back over at Sheriff Brady. He seemed not even to notice what was going on. Instead, he was eating his eggs.

Taking her cue from him, she took a sip of her coffee and tried to ignore the men. It was a little hard when the one stood up and stormed out the door. She met Brady's eyes over the rim of her cup and he winked. "It happens all the time."

Okay. So maybe she wouldn't have breakfast here again. Or maybe there was something she could do for the two men. She noticed that the one man, Stanley, continued to sit in his seat, contentedly eating sunflower seeds and spitting the husks into a bucket. Yuck! But at least it wasn't that tobacco stuff.

Sam brought her eggs and bacon and a refill of coffee for her and the sheriff. "Stanley, when you ever going to quit doing that to the man?"

"What was that?"

"You heard me. I saw you turn up your hearin' aid when Miss Dottie walked in."

Stanley frowned. His entire face dipping in a cascade of wrinkles, he punctuated the frown by spitting out another husk. "App needs his blood pressure raised once a year. Keeps him kickin'."

"Yeah, well, when he comes in here one day and kicks your—well, I ain't goin' there 'cause we have a lady in our presence, but you know what I'm talkin' about. I ain't gonna feel sorry for you at-*tal*."

Dottie watched Sam retreat behind the swinging doors. She was beginning to worry about the two gentlemen; she certainly couldn't eat. And then suddenly the door opened and Applegate strode back in, sat back down and grabbed a handful of seeds like nothing had happened.

"You old fool," he said. "I was halfway to my truck when I remembered what day it was."

"I get you every year." Stanley chuckled and rubbed his hands together.

Applegate frowned. Dottie couldn't help but think the man looked like a prune. Poor man. "You just wait till next April Fools' day. I'm gonna git you next year."

"Ain't happened yet."

April Fools'! Dottie couldn't believe she'd forgotten today was the first day of April. Sheriff Brady was smiling when she looked back at him.

"Whew, I thought they were really breaking up a longtime friendship," she said. This time she was the one leaning over the table.

"It happens every year. Keeps them alive, anyway. You better eat those eggs before they get cold and Sam gets upset with you."

Dottie grimaced, said a quick silent prayer then lifted her fork and dug in. Mule Hollow was truly starting out as an interesting place to spend a few days.

And she'd been here less than twelve hours.

"So, you were on your way to California before you picked Cassie up?"

"That's right. My brother is a pastor in Los Angeles and he's involved with a foundation for women at risk—battered women, unwed mothers. I spent two weeks at the place and now I'm moving out there to be kind of a housemother to them." Just thinking about it always made a happy face in her heart, not that it was a mother's role she would be

45

playing, but more that of a survivor and mentor. Someone who'd been down a similar road. "I'm going to keep the place up and teach the ladies some business skills. The plan is for me to reopen my candy business there and employ the women on a rotating basis. I can't wait."

Sheriff Brady placed his elbows on the table, linked his hands and rested his chin on his thumbs. "That's a great plan. You have a great heart."

Dottie shook her head. "When you've looked death in the face like I have and God brings you through... let me tell you, it'd be weird not to want to give back. I'm just making good on a promise I made to Him."

"Like I said, you have a good heart. Thousands of people make that same promise when faced with trying times. But as soon as they're back on their feet, they forget about it."

Thinking back to those dark hours before she was rescued, Dottie shuddered. "I'll never forget about what God delivered me from. Never. I look at life in an entirely new light. And I'm trying my hardest to live life in a new light." And she was. No looking back. Only up. Even the nightmare's return couldn't change that.

When she left the diner, Brady walked with her. As they approached the RV she was surprised to see cowboys everywhere working on different projects. It looked like a scene from *Lonesome Dove.*

And Cassie was right in the big middle of it. The kid was flitting from one group to the next, introducing herself and offering her hand in introduction. It looked suspiciously like speed dating.

"I wonder if any of those guys know what she's up to?"

"Oh, most of these guys are ready to settle down. Maybe not the younger ones, but for the most part all of them are thrilled with this campaign to get women out here to them. The odds of finding a wife out in this town looked pretty dismal after a while. Many of the guys actually had to move on to other places because they refused to live alone. Or shall we say they refused to live bunked up with a bunch of other rowdy bachelors for the rest of their lives."

Dottie couldn't blame them. But still, watching the serious look in Cassie's eyes, she couldn't help feeling the girl was looking at this as if she was picking out a pair of shoes or something. And that just wasn't right. Dottie had never been in love, but she wanted the man God intended for her to marry. That would be the most important thing she could look for but undeniably there would have to be chemistry between them. One didn't just stand the men up in a line and say that's him. There had to be more to it than that and she hoped Cassie would realize this and take her time looking for Mr. Right.

Sheriff Brady came to a halt in front of her RV. He placed his hands on his hips, emphasizing his broad shoulders and lean, muscular build. Dottie found herself studying his profile.

Why wasn't this guy married?

He was good-looking, nice, seemed great on the outside…and, well…

Oh, come on, Dottie! Get honest here.

All right already, she grumbled to herself. The man had chemistry coming out his ears. His name was probably listed under the word in the dictionary.

He seemed to have it all, and yet he was still single.

What did that mean?

CHAPTER FOUR

It was only eight o'clock in the morning, but after the hour spent at the diner, it felt much later. Now standing beside her RV with Sheriff Brady, Dottie was bewildered by her reactions to the man.

Flustered, she tugged open the RV's door and grabbed her bag of candy from the dash. Despite the heavy breakfast she'd eaten she needed to settle her nerves and to focus. And that meant sugar!

"Want one?" She held out the half-full bag of colorful gelatin-looking bunnies.

"No, thanks," Brady said, looking as if she'd offered him a bag of worms.

"Don't tell Sam," she whispered, plopping a couple into her mouth and letting the tangy little treats melt away.

"Your secret is safe with me," he said, dipping his

chin. "You do know that kind of stuff will kill you."

"Mmm, thanks for the warning. I'll keep that in mind the next time I get the urge to down the entire bag in one sitting."

His eyebrows met in a V. "Tell me you don't do that." She tried to look ashamed.

She really tried. And maybe she should actually be ashamed.

"Come on, tell me you haven't eaten an entire bag of those things!"

"Well..." She fidgeted from foot to foot. "Sometimes. But not often," she said, rapid-fire, gushing, and maybe feeling just a tad ashamed. "I want to live a long life. I just have to have a few of these a day."

Liar.

He shook his head and the corners of his lips lifted ever so slightly in that cute way of his. Pushing his hat back, he stared up at the top of the RV. It was obviously an attempt to hide the full-blown grin Dottie could see building. "How'd you get all of that up there?" he asked.

She smushed a bunny between her fingers and held it out to him in an audacious attempt to make him break into a full-out smile. He complied instead with a scowl, which was acceptable, too, and she rewarded herself promptly for having achieved said goal by tossing the yellow bunny into her own mouth with learned accuracy. Two points! *Yesss!*

"Believe me," she said before chewing. "It was not easy. Thank goodness a couple of friends from church helped me get the heavy stuff up there. I added a few other things after they went home. You should have seen us getting that wicker love seat up there."

She dipped into the bag again.

"Would you like some help getting it down?" Dottie halted her foraging. He really needed to go.

She was enjoying their conversation a little more than she wanted to. Okay, a whole lot more than she wanted to.

But she did need help. "The ladder is on the back."

He grinned. "No kidding."

"Sorry, I guess that would be the obvious place for it to be."

"Yu*uu*p," he said with an exaggerated Texas twang. He was still grinning at her when she looked up at him and their eyes locked. And she could almost hear thunder.

Chemistry!

"I'll be right down," he said, his penetrating gaze roaming her face before locking with her eyes again. He grabbed the metal ladder. It looked flimsy beneath his hands.

"Maybe I should go up," she said, sitting down her bag of bunnies on the bumper and making a move to grab the rungs. Their hands touched briefly and the tension that she'd been trying to ignore zinged to life. Chemistry! The obnoxious little voice in her head shouted. The voice she'd squish like a Gummi Bunny if she could get hold of it for all of its bouncing back and forth.

"No way are you going up there," he was saying. "Not while I'm around." He placed his hands on her shoulders and moved her to the side. "You wait right there."

Looking like a man who could handle anything, especially an itty-bitty bit of furniture on top of an RV, he climbed up the ladder and stepped onto the roof.

"I used to watch reruns of *Trapper John M.D.* when I was a kid and they used to climb on top of Gonzo's RV all the time, but this sure feels shaky."

That's putting it mildly, she thought, thinking about how she felt watching him. "There were three of us up there when we packed it up," she said, finding her voice.

"Then I'll have to trust you on that." He took a careful step toward the chaotic pile, then crouched down to loosen the ties.

Dottie watched, unable to not be interested. The man was just too cute when he concentrated. She squinted up at him in the morning sunlight and decided that he could take his time. She was just fine with the view.

He was pulling the rope from the racks when she caught a flash of pink in her peripheral vision. Turning, she saw a pink convertible Caddy bouncing and weaving across the pasture. The smiling blonde behind the wheel was waving one hand above her head and steering with the other as she brought the car to an abrupt halt.

"I heard you were here! Hello, hello, *helllooo,*" she laughed, vaulting out of the car and wrapping Dottie in a bear hug. Tightly. "I'd have come last night but I couldn't...we got tied up delivering the cutest little baby calf you ever laid your eyes on. But I told Clint, first thing this morning I was jumping in the Caddy and zooming right on over here to see about these two gals who decided to check out our little town. I'm hoping you're going to stay awhile. How are you? Did they get you set up good? Do you need anything?"

The woman paused her chattering, released Dottie and took a step back, hand extended. Dottie took it, staggered by the exuberant greeting. Thankful she hadn't had a Gummi Bunny in her mouth. She'd probably choke on it.

"Lacy Brown," the woman started again, then laughed, holding up her left hand and wiggling her wedding-banded finger. "I do that all the time. Lacy *Matlock* would be my name."

Lacy giggled and Dottie joined her, breaking her daze. She got the impression that around Lacy, laughter would be unending.

"Lacy, this is Dottie Hart," Brady said. "Dottie, Lacy has the tendency to talk a person to death if one isn't careful to escape when given the chance."

"So, Dottie, I hear Brady rescued you yesterday. That's our sheriff. Always rescuing someone. Never to be rescued himself."

"You can go home now, Lacy," Brady called down.

"Hey, no need to get mean."

"I just thought Clint might be missing you. That's all I meant."

"Uh-huh. And my hair is straight as a board."

Dottie looked at Lacy's nearly white hair sticking from her yellow hat in wild loose curls.

"I think he's pulling your leg," she said.

"You think?" Lacy asked, plopping a hand to her jutting hip.

"Has to be, because your hair is most definitely not straight."

Lacy chuckled. "I like you."

Dottie liked her, too. Who wouldn't? No wonder the town looked like it did with all its crayon colors. Lacy Matlock epitomized the phrase "colorful character."

"Ahh-hemmm."

Dottie looked up to see Brady holding a wicker chair over the edge of the RV for someone to take. "You girls going to stand there bonding all day, or are you going to give a poor fellow a helping hand."

Dottie looked at Lacy. "I guess we should help him."

"If you say so," Lacy sighed. "But I'm all for leaving him up there when we finish and us girls hanging out for a while."

Dottie agreed, then reached to take the chair and almost dropped it when Brady winked at her.

"I saw that, Brady Cannon," Lacy said.

Dottie knew she was pinker than the Caddy sitting behind her. A wink. What was that all about? He'd done the same thing in the diner, but she'd ignored it. But this time…she realized he was smiling down at her, almost laughing.

The man was playing with her, which she could take. The trouble was *Lacy Brown-Matlock!*

She'd witnessed the wink and she was smiling. Big.

And Dottie wasn't sure what, exactly, that smile meant...

Drawn by the pink Caddy, Cassie came running. Lacy made an instant friend by offering her a spin in her retro car. With the top down. Dottie had visions of Cassie coming back with her hair standing out like a rock stars.

"Those two will get along like peanut butter and jelly," Brady said, coming to stand beside her as she watched them driving off. Their arms touched and Dottie stepped away, startled at the sudden warm contact. "I hope so," she said. "Cassie's going to need a friend."

"Hey, she's going to be fine. As a matter of fact, the morning's gotten away from me, so I'm going to head to the office and start sending out some feelers. I'll let you know the minute I hear something."

"Thank you, that would be great," she said, almost forgiving him for the wink and the turmoil he caused her. "Who is that?" she asked, nodding toward the three ladies drawing close across the stretch of grass.

Brady glanced in their direction and smiled, watching their approach. "That's the heart of Mule Hollow. See you later. Hello, ladies, this is Dottie

Hart," he said, meeting them as he left. "Go easy on her, her RV's broke down and she has no escape." With that, he turned back toward her, tipped his hat at her, winked again and strode away.

Watching him leave, Dottie couldn't help thinking that George Strait had nothing on Brady Cannon. Brady's swagger was just as good as any cowboy she'd ever seen...George included.

"He's a cute one, our sheriff," the short lady with the curly gray hair said, crossing her arms and watching him walk away.

Dottie realized what she'd been doing and turned to the ladies. "Yes, he's extremely helpful."

"We know that for certain. Hi, I'm Norma Sue Jenkins."

"And I'm Esther Mae Wilcox," said the redhead. "You can like Brady. Really. We've been looking for the right woman for him for a while now. We thought it might be Ashby Templeton, but those two ended up knowing that they weren't a match after spending just one day at the fair together."

"Esther, don't push. Dottie has just arrived in Mule Hollow. And we're glad you're here. I'm Adela Ledbetter."

Dottie barely heard the smart-looking woman with the feathery white hair and the brilliant blue eyes. Her head was still spinning from what Ethel—*Es*ther— had said.

"Adela, I know she just arrived here," Esther continued. "But, from what I hear, she's not staying very long, so we need to move fast. You know, get her while the irons on fire."

"That's while the iron's hot," Norma added dryly.

"Hot, on fire, it's all the same thing. We just need to get her."

Dottie was grateful she hadn't passed out at the onslaught of the conversation. Instead, it was so shockingly comical, she chuckled.

"Why's that funny?"

Biting back the last of the giggle and feeling like Lucy, she blinked at Esther. "Well, ma'am. I'm not here looking for a husband. I'm just passing out—I mean through."

"And—what's your point?"

Dottie looked at the other two ladies, who had given up trying to contain their friend. "Well, I—"

"Me and my Hank, it just took a look and a wink and we were together for life."

"I thought it was a kiss?" Norma Sue said.

"Well, that, too. But I knew before that."

"Okay, Esther," Adela said, smiling. "Let's do like Brady asked and give the poor girl a little room. If it's to happen it will."

"Honestly, I'm leaving," Dottie blurted. These women were serious about their matchmaking. Give them an inch and wham!

Then it hit her. Again. Brady Cannon had *known*.

He'd known *exactly* what he was doing when he'd left her to fend for herself!

And the wink! Winks!

Ohhh, he was devious. The man had set the hounds on her on purpose. But why? What would possess him to do such a thing?

Looking from one pleasant-faced woman to the next, for the life of her she couldn't understand why he would do this…unless he was just being funny.

Funny, my foot! She'd get him for this.

Back at his office, Brady was hoping something would come up fast and the case would be a snap. A database search was the place to start.

He knew it was too much to hope for that she'd simply run away from home because of something trivial. He knew the odds were against it. On the flip side, he hoped she wasn't on the run because of something she'd done. It was a logical possibility.

For all involved, the sooner he found out the facts

relating to Cassie the better. The last thing he needed was for her to win the hearts of all the townsfolk only to do something to harm them.

And then there was Dottie. It wasn't like he went around winking at women all the time. It just happened. He had nothing to gain by it.

Besides, for all he knew, Dottie's story could be false. Hey, she and Cassie could be involved in something together…con artists came in all shapes and ages. And the good women of Mule Hollow would be easy game.

Clenching his jaw Brady picked up a pen from his desk and rolled it between his thumb and forefinger. His gut tightened and he told himself he was being ridiculous. He understood where the tendency came from, a man who'd seen it all and heard it all grew cynical.

He gave the pen tip three hard strikes to his desktop.

You're not that guy anymore. Remember.

For a while, in the city, he'd lived on the excitement. The fast-paced rhythm of the precinct, the city lights, the adrenaline rush that came with every bust…

He closed his eyes, tightening his fingers around the pen…

I can do all things through Christ, who strengthens me.

Dottie's words...good, open-hearted Dottie. Just thinking of her prompted a smile. He was a cop. His duty demanded that he check all details. Pick up on all possible angles.

In his old life, everyone was a suspect—he closed his eyes—but not anymore.

Dottie Hart was the real deal. He knew it and he refused to allow his fight with his past taint what he knew was true.

He opened his eyes. So why had he flirted with her? *Because you couldn't help it. Something about her, the inner beauty that radiated from her reached out to him.*

Leaning back in his chair, he stared up at the ceiling and refocused on the problem at hand. Cassie.

It was true there could be any assortment of horrible reasons that the girl had been hitchhiking yesterday. But there was still a small ray of hope that everything she'd told Dottie was true. That she'd really come to Mule Hollow because of Molly's articles.

He prayed that this was the case.

Not to mention how happy it would make the matchmaking posse of Mule Hollow.

CHAPTER FIVE

The welcome committee had grown to include several other women by the time Lacy and Cassie came rolling back in the Caddy.

"We're not gonna let you girls leave here," Esther Mae declared as Dottie set a pan of fresh fudge on the table that now had a rug beneath it and flowers in its center. "You two fit in with us like peas in a pod."

"That's right," Norma Sue agreed. "Why, the moment Sam told Adela you were here and Adela called me, I had a good feeling."

Dottie laughed. "I thanked the Lord for letting me break down in such a nice place." She was trying not to think about what was cooking in their one-track minds.

"I think that's so neat the way you followed Molly's stories, Cassie," Lilly Wells said, giving the girl a thumbs-up. "You just might find yourself a cowboy, if you really want one."

"I'm glad my articles are making an impact," Molly Popp added, flipping her rust-colored hair over her shoulder before placing a piece of fudge on her napkin. "I'm having unbelievable fun writing those stories. And the response has been overwhelming."

"The post office has never seen so much mail," Esther Mae added. "Hon, this fudge is so good my hips are expanding just smelling the stuff. And I don't even give a hoot."

Lacy's nail tech, Sheri Marsh, paused before shoving a huge piece of extra-dark fudge into her mouth. "Where did you learn to make this? You need to know that I might be skinny, but I'm training to be a professional eater. And I think I just discovered my competitive food category." She laughed and finished off the hunk of candy.

Dottie was amazed. Lacy had introduced her as the only woman she could think of who would've dropped everything to drive five hundred miles for a cup of coffee and the chance to share an adventure with her. Dottie had a vivid picture in her mind of the two of them riding cross-country in the Caddy. It wouldn't have been boring, of that she was certain. And for the life of her, she didn't know where all that fudge was going! Sheri was about the size of Olive Oyl and she'd put away at least six pieces of the rich stuff.

That in itself was a testament to her grandma Sylvia's candy-making talent. Dottie was embarrassed to accept all the praise the fudge was getting. She loved to cook, and had loved having her shop. Its reputation had grown so that she'd been able to make a nice profit from its sale. The money was enough to get her set up in California, but she still felt like an impostor when people complimented her cooking abilities.

"My grandma and Mom passed their talent and love of cooking down to me. And their recipes," she said, giving credit where it was due.

"Really," Lacy said, tapping her tangerine fingernails on the tabletop. "You know, Mule Hollow could use a good restaurant. Have you thought about that possibility? Just don't do an all-you-can-eat buffet— Sheri'd bankrupt you."

Dottie tugged at her earlobe, perplexed by their inability to hear any phrase resembling "no."

"Well, um, like I said, I have obligations to fulfill elsewhere. Though I dearly love Mule Hollow, I really do. I'm opening an old-fashioned candy store in California."

Norma Sue was watching her. And Dottie saw her exchange a look with Esther Mae. They were at it again, despite what she'd just said. They hadn't heard the no again.

"Sam told me Brady was bragging on you this morning. Said you were an unusual woman to go out of your way to bring Cassie here."

"She is," Cassie blurted out. Plopping a hand over her fudge-filled mouth, she continued talking. "I never dreamed anyone would bring me all the way here. I think she's wonderful. I was afraid I was going to have to either walk all the way or endure a ride with a jerk or two. I vote you stay here. With us." She smiled and there was chocolate on her front teeth. It was not a pretty sight, but it touched Dottie's heart, and despite her discomfort she wanted to hug the kid.

She thanked God once more for placing her on that road at the right time to pick Cassie up.

Adela patted Cassie's hand, a serene smile lighting her expression, her eyes so full of wisdom it radiated from her. "God has a way of putting people exactly where He wants them. Although, your hitchhiking disturbs me greatly, young woman, I'm glad you're here.

"No offense, Miss Adela," Cassie said, "but I'm not real sure about the God stuff."

Dottie looked around at the lovely women—*pushy deaf women, true,* but she knew that if any group of women could help Cassie understand that *the God stuff*

65

was *the good stuff* it would be this group.

This was a group of women who could truly have an impact upon women in need. The thought dug into her heart and started to germinate.

"Dottie, why don't you tell us about this mission you're on," Lacy said.

Dottie met her gaze. This was a woman who knew about missions. Her coming to Mule Hollow had been a complete stepping out on faith, her own mission. Suddenly Dottie couldn't help herself.

"God has opened doors for me in California. No Place Like Home is the shelter for women in crisis, and it's struggling financially. My brother needs me." Dottie frowned thinking about it. Glancing around at the interest she saw on everyone's faces, she continued, actually relieved to talk about it with someone.

"They've lost funding, you see, due to cutbacks, and unless they find a way to gain that income back, the shelter could fold. And it can't. It just can't. You should see the women who live there. Stacy, for one. She's the sweetest woman, has a baby, and because of her child, she left behind a chronic history of abuse. She had been abused all her childhood, then married a man who did the same. She found the courage to seek help after she gave birth."

"Bless her heart," Norma Sue said, shaking her head.

Dottie nodded. "She has no skills, she rarely speaks, but she's hanging on. The shelter cannot close. God has given me a reason for having lived…" She paused, not wanting to go into detail about herself. This was not about her, but her friends in California. "Anyway, much is riding on my plan. If all goes well, the income from the candy store we open could support the house. Make it self-sufficient." Helping them achieve a better life would be a wonderful defining moment in her life. What could be better than taking a woman with a broken spirit and no hope and helping her find a new life path?

"Dottie, it sounds fantastic! My blood gets fired up thinking about ministry."

"Oh, girl, *pul-ease* do believe her when she says that," Sheri said.

Lacy slapped Sheri's knee. "Like you aren't. Ministry, any kind of ministry, here, there, it doesn't matter where, or what kind, as long as you're sharing God's love with others. There isn't a more rewarding calling."

"Of course, there are other factors working against us also," Dottie said. "The lease is coming up for renewal in three weeks and we're praying that the rent doesn't skyrocket. Or worse, get pulled. On top of that, my brother, Todd, has just learned that the owner has been made an offer he can't refuse by an investment group who wants to open a shopping center on the location." Dottie fought the anger that tried to overcome her every time she thought about it.

"I'm trying not to get too worried. I know God wouldn't allow this to happen," Dottie said. "No Place Like Home is a wonderful place. Rose, another resident, she's a single mom with a thirteen-year-old son… they lived in their car for two weeks before Todd found them. They were scared—" Dottie met the gazes of the ladies of Mule Hollow. Looking into their eyes, she saw the flame of compassion.

She was glad she'd come here. Mule Hollow was a perfect example of how the world could be if more people united in a common goal. It was an inspiration from the Lord; this place was a utopia she could try and recreate once she moved in with Rose and the others, and set her plan into action. She refused to worry. She would put her faith to action and know that God had a plan.

By the time the evening was rolling in on her first official day in Mule Hollow, Dottie had met so many people, so many new *friends,* she felt as if she'd lived in Mule Hollow all her life. The town was addictive. How could anyone come here and want to leave?

Dottie rose with the chickens on her second day in Mule Hollow. *Really,* the chickens were wandering around outside her trailer pecking at the grass like bobble-headed dolls. They were all colors. She'd never thought about a chicken, except when she was about to eat it. But chickens were very colorful, very different individuals.

She prepared her coffee and watched the funky fowl systematically peck and dash around looking for the bugs that would make their next treat. They were fun to watch and kind of pretty, as chickens go, with all of their various colors. It occurred to her that she might be turning into a redneck sitting there watching chickens. It also occurred to her that she was happy.

She hadn't had a nightmare, which greatly relieved her. Yesterday had been a weird and wonderful day. Yet when she'd planted her head on her pillow last night, she'd feared the nightmares would return—but no, God had been great and given her instead a peaceful night. Waking up to the chickens had been icing on the cake.

Reluctantly, she pulled herself away from the sight and prepared for the day of massive cooking. She had two days to cook; she figured she could get the candy all made up and then simply sell it during the festivities. But before she did anything, she sat down at her laptop computer, once again thankful for the satellite connection she'd invested in, and wrote her daily email to Todd, which he would pass along to Rose and the others at the house.

She'd been sending them e-mails about her cross country trip all the way. They loved it. None of them had ever been out of the city, most had lived within the same ten-mile radius all their lives. It was a given that they'd especially enjoyed hearing about Mule Hollow. The chickens were sure to be a hit, as were Lacy Matlock and Norma Sue and Esther Mae; they'd love everything. And though she'd only e-mailed a few times, some of the women were looking up Molly's back stories.

She might have to bring them all out to the tiny town for a visit.

Now, *there* was a thought.

Even if it was for just a couple of days, it would give them a different perspective on life.

The thought sent a warm fuzzy straight to her heart. She could just see them visiting here. The mental image she had of them being literally embraced by the people of this lovable town was so vivid, so real, it stunned her.

Immediately she dashed off a new e-mail to Todd and told him her thoughts. One day they might make it happen.

E-mail sent, she moved to start her candy assembly. According to Lacy, they were expecting a crowd of hundreds. So Dottie was thinking big. She was going to prepare more fudge, a herd of brownies with nuts and without, her favorite coconut balls with nuts...she'd love to make peanut brittle because it was always a great seller, but there was no way the RV could handle such a job. She'd have to settle on the basic moneymakers. And maybe she could get some Gummi Bunnies in, too.

Out of nowhere, Sheriff Brady stepped into her thoughts and started winking and waving. She mentally pushed the good-looking lawman away. No matter how much he waved, the big hunk of a man could jump up and down, even stand on his head, she was not getting sidetracked thinking about how nice he was. Or how nice his smile was, or how... Okay, that was enough of that. Enough!

"What time is it?" Cassie moaned.

"It's five-thirty, sleepyhead," she laughed,

glancing at the groggy-eyed, hairy monster leering down at her from the bunk. Glad to have something else to think about.

"Why are you up so early?" Cassie mumbled into her pillow.

"Because we've got candy to make! Jump into the shower and then you can help me."

An eye blinked at Dottie from beneath the pillow. "Up, me?"

"Well, yea-*ah.*"

Cassie pushed the pillow off her head and crawled down off the bunk, squeezed past Dottie and disappeared into the compact shower. No complaints. Dottie was impressed.

The girl's parents had to be going crazy missing her.

Surely Brady had found something out; she'd forgive him for the winks if he'd learned anything, anything at all about Cassie.

Moving quickly, she organized the ingredients for her first batch of goodies, then prepared the table with the cellophane paper and ribbon that she would have Cassie cut for wrapping the candy. All the while, her mind kept looping back to thoughts of Brady, like an eight-second video feed that refused to rest. Drat the man.

He'd said she had a good heart. That pleased her.

She did want people to notice that God had placed within her a changed heart. That He had made a difference in her. But the human side of her was pleased that Brady had noticed and liked what he saw. That was the part that kept bugging her. Why did his noticing please her so much?

Carefully she began measuring sugar into a large mixing bowl and then went on autopilot as she continued her task, a task she'd done many times over her lifetime. Memories of baking with her mother and grandmother always brought a smile to her lips.

"Hey, that water felt *goood!*" Cassie squealed, bursting from the shower wrapped in a towel.

Dottie laughed. "You must be feeling better."

"Oh, yes. Let me put my clothes on and then you can put me to work."

Dottie watched her disappear into the back bedroom, where she'd stored her clothes. She said a prayer of thanksgiving once again and prayed Brady had gotten a hit on her background.

They'd been working for three straight hours when nine o'clock rolled around and Cassie popped from her chair. "Hey! A jumping jungle!"

"What?" Dottie looked up from adding dry

ingredients together in a large pot to follow Cassie's gaze out the window toward a lump of heavy plastic a group had gathered around. "How do you know what that is?"

"Because I helped. I mean, we always had them in—I've seen them everywhere. Hey, Jake's out there."

And she was gone, just as Dottie opened her mouth to warn against chasing after Jake too hard. The girl was quick on the go, she'd give her that.

Watching her jog across the pasture, Dottie's attention snagged on Sheriff Brady stepping from his truck near the gathering group. He glanced toward her RV and her heartbeat kicked up a notch. A big notch.

Really, Dottie, you're being ridiculous.

This infatuation with Brady couldn't continue. She knew this and yet she had to fight the urge to follow Cassie.

It was foolhardy, this romantic revelation her heart was having. She had an agenda and nothing was going to stand in her way.

She dumped the water into the dry ingredients, which thanked her for dumping on them by exploding in a white cloud that whooshed right back at her. Coughing, she ignored the mess and started stirring with a vengeance. Maybe that was what was wrong with Brady.

She was just too gullible. She really didn't have much experience with men. It wasn't as if she ever dated much. What did she know? Really.

Besides, she couldn't go off and leave candy standing. Candy had to be tended carefully. She started stirring again. She owed him for winking at her the way he'd done—so she needed to come up with some payback.

That was exactly what she needed to do. She snatched the bag of peanuts, ripped it open and doused the mixture with them. There, take *that,* Brady Cannon, ya big flirt—and I hope you choke—

A soft rap on the door interrupted her diabolical plan.

"Dottie, are you in there?" Brady's deep voice called through the screen and she nearly choked.

Forgive me, Lord…I didn't really mean I was going to…well, You know—choke him.

Her guilty gaze darted to the counter, for what she wasn't sure, there was no evidence linking her to the peanut assault she'd been engaging in. He wouldn't know that she'd mentally just tossed a bag of nuts on him. Or envisioned him with chocolate dripping down his face. *Or hoped he choked—she was so bad!*

"Dottie."

"Come in. I can't stop what I'm doing at the

moment." She felt sick, suddenly nervous, kind of feverish...*humiliated* was the word. She set the mixture on the stove and stirred like she had a bionic arm.

Like she was getting rid of the evidence.

The fact that she had the hairnet on hit her a little too late.

"I smell chocolate," he said in that voice that was low and edgy like the bass on the radio turned up just a bit higher than the treble.

She sighed when he stepped into the RV, standing on the lower of the two steps leading up into the cabin. Bringing them to eye level in the cramped quarters...which was just way too agitating for a girl who had been having the crazy angst that she'd been suffering with for the last few minutes! All because of him. "Don't think you're getting any of this," she snapped. "Not after what you did."

"Hey, it was a joke."

"So you admit it!" She pointed the chocolate-covered spoon at him. "Do you *know* how much trouble you got me into?" His smile told her that he did, and that he was still full of more mischief. His gorgeous smile was enough to send her spinning, but she fought it off. "I'm about to drop hot chocolate clusters into these molds and can't stop at the moment.

So, buster, my hands are tied up right now. But you better watch your back, because we are not finished with this subject." She pointed the spoon at him again.

He spread his hands out open palmed. "Come on now, just think how happy it made them."

Dottie started spooning the clusters into the mold but paused to give him an annoyed look. "Oh, it made them happy all right. They practically have us married!"

He chuckled. "They are a tenacious lot. But on to the important question of the day... Can a community servant coax a fresh cluster out of the vengeful candy lady?"

Dottie's jaw dropped in disbelief. "Now you think I'm going to give you candy? Have you no shame?"

His grin said "not an ounce" as he stepped up into the room. She arched an eyebrow. "Hey, bud, I didn't say you could come in." She was flirting with the man. After all that she'd just put herself through, now she was flirting! What was wrong with her?

"But you didn't say I couldn't." He winked.

Dottie laughed, instantly defused. "You're terrible. Come in. If you dare."

He rubbed his hands together and smiled like a kid. His dark brown eyes glittered with good-hearted teasing. He took the seat that Cassie had vacated, but where Cassie had had plenty of room he had very little leeway. He was a very fit man, muscular and tall. Maybe he had a girlfriend! He might not be married, but he could be involved. The women of Mule Hollow might just think they knew everything but maybe they didn't. *Whoa, where did that come from? That is none of your concern. Winks or no winks. Only a few minutes ago you thought something was wrong with him.* She had never been so confused in all her life. "So how about that candy?"

"It might be arranged."

"How are you feeling today?"

"That's it!" She held up the wooden spoon again. "No talking about my health or there will not be any candy for you." Finished, she plunked the pot into the sink, then carefully stacked the molds and set them to the side to cool. Hoping to settle the rapid thumping of her heart, she took a deep breath before turning back toward Brady.

"I bet you were a terrible patient."

She dipped her chin and met his eyes and wished she hadn't been hurting the day she met him. But at least she had something else to focus on instead of her infatuation with him. "Actually, I had to endure people hovering over me for months. Thank goodness for them, I loved them all. But I'm good now. Everyone has twinges here and there. You just caught me in the middle of a twinge."

His lips curved at the edges just slightly as he rolled his shoulder and groaned. "Yeah, I had a twinge here in my shoulder this morning, but I slapped some horse liniment on it and it's gone now." He rubbed his shoulder. "If you need to borrow it I have plenty. I could trade it for some candy."

"Funny."

"No, really. It works great. Smells a little strong." He made a face, crinkling up his nose and lifting his eyebrows.

Dottie laughed, and slapped his shoulder with the dishrag from hers. "I think I'd better get you a piece of candy before I make you leave."

"Leave?"

"Yes, for misbehaving." She pried the top off a large candy tin and removed two pieces of chocolate with a napkin and placed them in front of him.

"You know, you might not ever get rid of me if I like this. I've heard rumors that it's unbelievable."

She smiled warmly, relaxing somewhat. "Then I guess I'm stuck with you because it is very unbelievable."

He laughed loudly and looked at her in disbelief. "Kinda full of yourself, are you?"

It dawned on her how her statement would have sounded to him and she blushed. "No! Not at all," she gasped, smiling despite her embarrassment. "The praise goes to my grandmother. This is her recipe passed down with careful training. That tiny piece of candy you're holding has won every blue ribbon it could possibly win at every county fair within ten counties of my hometown, not to mention all the state fairs it's won."

"Is that so." He turned the cluster over and studied it, his expression perplexed. "Exactly how old is this particular piece of candy?"

Dottie rolled her eyes, tempted to pop him with the towel again. "Anybody ever tell you that you're a wise guy?"

"You'd be the first."

"I don't believe that for a second. Wise guy."

Dottie was a breath of fresh air and he was a crazy man! Brady watched the way expressions played across her face and he was incapable of not teasing her. She'd been on his mind all night, good thoughts. One look at her this morning, with her sparkling eyes and soft smile, had him wondering how he'd even entertained darker thoughts about her.

Teasing her came naturally. It achieved a reaction that he liked…the way her eyes twinkled when she caught on that he was pulling her leg. He liked the way she adapted to the teasing. He kept remembering the look on her face when Stanley played the April Fools' joke on Applegate. She'd been so sure the two were really fighting. It had been priceless.

He took a bite of the candy. First the chocolate, then the caramel, so thick and rich, melted in his mouth. It was superb. "Okay, so how much for about twenty pounds of this stuff?"

"Find out about Cassie, and twenty pounds of candy is yours for free."

He swallowed the candy and studied the scene outside the window. Jake and Cassie were helping Esther Mae and Hank Wilcox get the inflatable play gym set up. The rest of the crowd had moved to other duties in preparation for the weekend. As he watched, Cassie placed her hand on Jake's arm and smiled up at the young cowboy, who responded with a smile that made him resemble a lovesick puppy.

"I'm expecting a fax from Austin. There was a report filed yesterday about a missing nineteen-year-old. She's been missing for four days."

Dottie's expression saddened. "I just don't get it. What would make a kid like Cassie leave her home?" Twisting the dishrag with both hands, she sat down carefully across the table from him and watched the

81

kids through the window. "She's a great kid—young woman. I mean, at first I thought she was going to be a pain, but I think that was just her fear of being picked up by the wrong person on the highway. I mean, she was fascinating, the way she talked about Mule Hollow all the way here. She adores this place, but surely the girl didn't run away from home just to find a husband. Look at her. She's as cute and fresh as they come."

"Hey…Dottie…" Brady reached and covered her increasingly agitated hands with his. Immediately she ceased wringing the life out of the towel and looked at him. "She's a good kid. It's easy to see that. I've seen kids in the city run away for all kinds of reasons. The stories don't always turn out to be bad. Believe me, this may be nothing."

He prayed he was giving her encouragement that had merit.

"When do you think you'll know more?"

"The information may be in my office now. Why don't you ride over there with me. It won't take long. I'll also be getting a rundown on names, too. Bates is a fairly common name and I have a feeling that Cassie is a nickname."

She glanced over at the counter that was covered with ingredients and bowls. It was a small space, but she'd managed to make it work. He could see her mind churning.

"Okay, I can start packaging the candy I've made so far after we check on this. Finding out about Cassie is a priority."

"Then let's go."

He watched as she stood up, placing her hands on the tabletop then pressing firmly with her palms to give support as she rose. She removed the green apron she wore and pulled the funny net off her head. Her silky hair flowed about her shoulders as she smiled sheepishly up at him.

"I forgot I had this fancy hat on."

"I thought you looked pretty cute in it."

"A wise guy and a fibber." Her cheeks grew pink.

"Let's not be spreading that about. Most folks believe everything I tell them."

She followed him into the midmorning sunshine. "Is that so?"

He laughed. "Well, I am the sheriff."

"Precisely why I'm not holding my observations against you."

He was about to throw a teaser back at her when Esther Mae saw them.

"Hello, you two."

"Hello, Esther Mae, Hank," he said, reaching into the cab of his truck and retrieving his hat. He'd removed it earlier thinking he was going to be tussling with the inflatable. Settling it back on his head, he felt complete again.

"It looks like everything's going along really well," Dottie said. Her shoulder touched his arm as she paused beside him, instantly distracting Brady. She smelled of vanilla and chocolate and that was a combination that would do any man in.

"It's going great," he heard Esther saying. Brady glanced down at Dottie's shiny black hair then back to Esther. It wouldn't do to feed their speculations.

"And how is our good sheriff treating you today?" Esther's eyes widened and she lifted an eyebrow and he realized the older woman hadn't missed anything. At least Dottie wasn't aware of anything.

Or was she? Watching color seep into Dottie's pale skin again, he wasn't sure if it was embarrassment or just the warmth of the morning sunshine. She had been through a terrible ordeal and he had to pull back his infatuation and remember she needed some looking after. He had to remember to try and get her out into the sun a little bit. After going through such a rigorous recovery, she needed the outdoors to finish her therapy. There was nothing like a good hike to strengthen stamina and give a healthy glow. The glow she was wearing now was *not* normal.

She looked up at him and caught him red-handed staring at her.

"I think he studied the manual last night. Sheriff Brady is treating me in strict accordance with the Mule Hollow hospitality regulations."

Esther laughed and gave them both a funny squinty-eyed going-over that made Brady more nervous.

"Of that I was pretty certain," she said. "Our Brady is a very smart man. Remember that."

Brady tugged at his collar. "Dottie, I think we'd better go over there and look at those ideas—"

"Oh, yes. Sure. I'll talk to you later, Esther. Bye, Hank."

"Bye, now, we'll have this little rubber ducky done when you get back and maybe you can join Jake and Cassie on the first bounce."

Dottie glanced toward the back of the "little rubber ducky" as Hank had called it, and waved at Cassie as she guided a portion of the rapidly swelling thing to its position. "I don't think I want to do that."

"Sure you do. It'll be fun."

Brady saw the fear that flickered across Dottie's face. "If we're not back in time, maybe we can do it later."

"Sure," Hank said.

"That'll be better anyway, Brady. You can catch 'er

if she falls," Esther Mae said.

Brady nodded and opened his truck door. It was time to get out of the fire. There was something cooking. He could tell it by the look in Esther Mae's eyes. Maybe he shouldn't have winked at Dottie in front of the ladies. It had been a spur-of-the-moment act...but he might live to regret it, because he got the distinct impression that something was simmering and he'd single-handedly hurled himself and Dottie right smack into the middle of the frying pan.

Where exactly had his brains gone?

CHAPTER SIX

"It's not her." Holding the picture of the Austin runaway in her hands, Dottie raised her distraught gaze. "Oh, how I hate life sometimes. I wish I could fix this."

Brady took the picture and placed it on his desk. "We can't fix everything, but we can try and make a difference when we can. What you're doing for Cassie is more than two-thirds of the population would do."

"I hope the percentage is more than that. Surely more than two-thirds would reach out a hand to someone in need."

Brady shrugged. Truth was truth.

The phone rang and his gaze followed Dottie as she walked to the wall of pictures, giving him some privacy as he picked up the receiver.

"Sheriff's office," he said, watching Dottie, her hair

moving in a silky mass as she leaned in to study the photos on the wall.

He turned away and asked Seth Turner to repeat himself. There had been a wreck on one of the county roads twelve miles outside of town.

The truck driver was trapped inside his cab.

Dottie knew by the sound of Brady's voice that something bad had happened. She swung around just as he was hanging up the phone and shoving back from the desk to stand. The change was instantaneous.

Suddenly the low-key Brady was gone. The man rounding the edge of the desk was a man on a mission. Dottie had learned heros lurked inside the mildest-looking men and women. Of course, Brady already wore a uniform. He was no surprise. It was those who'd saved her who had been the surprise.

And forever opened her eyes.

"There's been an accident. I'm sorry to cut this short."

"Can I come? I promise to stay out of the way."

She followed him from the building, dismayed at his hesitation. "C'mon, you might need me."

He paused slightly in the street, as if assessing her ability. She realized the last thing he needed was to take someone to an accident site who might fall apart. Freak at the sight of blood or something.

"I can do this, Brady." She met his eyes head-on and nodded hard to reassure his searching gaze. It was obvious that he had grown used to assessing situations and making split-second decisions.

"Load up."

Yessss!

Within seconds they were flying out of town, lights flashing, siren blaring and Dottie's heart pounding double time. It hadn't occurred to her that she might not be able to handle what she was about to encounter. Until it was too late. What if she weren't… What if she couldn't… Her stomach rolled just thinking about actually stepping up to the plate and delivering on her promise.

What if she was a coward?

Listening to Brady on the radio coordinating the different units needed in the rescue distracted her, brought her out of her sudden worries.

He was wonderful. She watched him, precise, direct, ready for anything he would find upon arrival.

A man's life could depend on him.

Dottie sucked in a calming breath. The scenery sped by as she focused and prayed for the man who was trapped in the overturned truck. Thanked God for the competent man sitting beside her. How she could have thought anything bad about him only an hour earlier was a total bafflement to her. He was great through and through.

The eighteen-wheeler had turned over out in the middle of nowhere. Seth had seen the accident happen from his tractor, but because of the unreliability of cell phones in the area he'd been forced to drive to his house to call it in.

When they arrived on the scene, a cowboy jogged toward them.

"That's Seth," Brady said, opening his door almost before the truck slammed to a halt. He'd filled her in on all the details, all business, and now he took charge just as he had when her RV caught fire.

It was more than obvious that Seth was distraught, but his relief clearly won out when Brady stepped from his truck. She understood the feeling. Brady Cannon looked as if he could handle anything.

She followed them to the crash, hanging back, though, not wanting to get in the way as Brady assessed the situation then talked calmly to the poor man inside the crushed cab. He was bleeding badly, but conscious. Brady instructed Seth on how to hold the man's head straight to protect against further damage in case of a neck injury, then he motioned for her to come forward. Pulling absorbent pads from the kit he'd carried to the truck with him, he laid them across the cut on the man's head.

"I need you to hold this. It needs pressure. Can you do this?"

There was blood everywhere. She swallowed hard, nodded. The man was lying at an odd angle, he blinked at her as she scooted into the tight quarters beside Seth. "Y'all are doing great," Brady told the two of them and then he reached in and touched the trucker's shoulder. "Paul, this is Seth and Dottie. You talk to them while I get to work on getting your legs free so when the cavalry arrives we can be ready to transport you." Paul's frightened gaze settled on Dottie as memories flooded into her mind. Cold darkness, no room to breathe, no way to move as liquid dripped into her face from broken water pipes mingling with her own blood... Dottie fought the need to run, the need to escape, to cry...her hands trembled against Paul's clammy skin and she was sure he could see her distress.

I am with you always.

Dottie focused. Remembering the promise God gave His people cut through her panic like a sail through stormy winds. She fought her fear of close confines.

You can do all things through Christ, who strengthens you. She focused on the verse pushing sense back into her panicked mind. She would not be beat. This was the nightmare that had plagued her for months, but there was no fleeing from it this time. No escape without leaving Paul behind. And that wasn't an option. She hadn't been left behind, and despite her fear, she refused to leave her post.

Locking into Paul's stricken eyes, she pressed the pads to his forehead and forced a smile. She would give him the same kind encouragement and help that her rescuers had given her.

Brady's hand on her shoulder centered her even further on the task at hand. She looked up to see him looking intently at her. Only a brief moment had passed since she'd scooted into the confines of the cab, but it had all moved in such slow motion that it felt like hours.

"You can do this. Keep him talking. I'll be back."

She watched him stride away then focused on Paul and nothing else.

Dottie watched Brady from her seat in the truck's cab. She was numb, her muscles ached from crouching in the same position for over an hour, but it was little sacrifice for the reward. The EMT had said things looked good for Paul thanks to their actions. Dottie knew it was because of Brady that everything had gone the way it had. It turned out that she and Seth had had the easy jobs. It was Brady who'd saved the day.

While the ambulance drove off, Dottie watched Brady taking care of details, having the truck towed off, organizing the cleanup of the tons of grain spilled across the road.

She was impressed by Brady's professional manner and wondered again if Mule Hollow knew how lucky they were to have a man like him in their community.

She owed her life to men like Brady. Men who'd put their lives on the line to rescue others.

Fond thoughts replayed across her memory of the men who'd worked tirelessly for days trying to dig her from beneath the mass of crumbled brick, wood and mud.

Tears came to her eyes. Not one man who'd done that for her had been on a payroll. Volunteers one and all who'd worked without sleep and no pay for the hours they'd put in to save her.

Looking down, she realized her hands were shaking. She closed her eyes and hugged herself, loathing the weakness she felt as her entire body started to tremble. "He was a lucky man," Brady said as he climbed into the cab beside her.

Dottie nodded. Praying he wouldn't notice that she was struggling.

"Dottie—"

He was out of the truck and yanking her door open within seconds. Pulling her out into the fresh air and into the circle of his strong arms.

"C'mon, you're okay," he whispered into her hair.

He held her hard, almost as if he was willing his strength to flow into her. She fought to find a foothold on that strength. But memories, like a landslide, took her back to the pit, to the grave that plagued her, and she wept.

And Brady held her.

What had he been thinking? The woman had lived through a nightmare and he'd brought her to a life-and-death situation and used her. She'd saved the day but at what cost?

He knew people who lived through horrifying experiences could carry that baggage with them for the rest of their lives. He shouldn't have let her come. He'd been careless.

"You were wonderful," she mumbled against his shirt after a few minutes. The dampness of her tears soaked to his heart.

He ran a hand down her silky hair and closed his eyes, trying to ignore the perfect way she seemed to fit in his arms. "No, you were. I know it was hard on you, but you were so strong for Paul. He needed all that encouragement you gave him. I hope someone did that for you." A sudden picture of Dottie covered in mud, buried in a hole, trapped and bleeding, slammed into him and he held her tighter.

She nodded against his shoulder. "They did. Two men tunneled to me. Even when they thought the building was going to cave in the rest of the way, they didn't abandon me. They literally were going to die with me if they had to. They said it had taken them too long to tunnel to me just to back out and leave me..." Her soft laugh was cut off by a hiccup. "They stayed and while they dug me out, they talked to me and kept the water out of my face..."

Her voice trailed off.

"And that's what you did for Paul today."

She relaxed against him. He could feel the strength flowing back into her. She was going to hate that she'd shown this weakness. She'd already shown him that she hated being fussed over.

"I was so afraid I was going to fail him."

Brady laughed and pushed her away from him so that he could look into her face. "Fail him? You were amazing. You knew exactly what to say to him. It was obvious you knew how he felt. I'm so sorry you had to go through such a terrifying ordeal, Dottie."

She wiped her eyes and stepped away from him. He hated to let her go. "Thank you. I didn't mean to fall apart. It's not like I was the only person to go through what I did. At least I lived…many didn't."

He lifted her chin with his finger. "I think you are working hard to give back. I admire what you're trying to do in California."

Looking at her bloodshot eyes, her puffy blotchy cheeks and her red nose, Brady couldn't tear his eyes away.

She was a mess! She was beautiful.

And he wanted to kiss her and never let her go.

CHAPTER SEVEN

Dottie could not believe Brady's kitchen. It was humongous.

Huu-mon-gous!

There were nearly four complete walls of cabinets, floor to ceiling, and counter space that went on and on and on. There was a six-burner gas stove just begging to be used and a double oven. She definitely could work here. After the rescue call, he'd insisted that she use his kitchen to get ready for the fair, pointing out that she needed more space if she was going to prepare adequately.

Reluctantly, she'd agreed. Now she was happy she'd accepted his offer. It wasn't a professional kitchen, but it was close.

"Hey, Dottie, look at this place!" Cassie exclaimed as she dropped a sack of decorations on the kitchen island then spun around in amazement. Dottie had already done the same thing.

"You live here all alone?" she asked Brady as he entered carrying an armload of bags.

"All alone."

"Whoa," Cassie gasped.

Dottie didn't miss the expression that passed over Brady's face. "Go check it out if you want to. My mom had it built to be enjoyed."

Cassie disappeared instantly through the doorway. "Do you have a lot of brothers and sisters?" Dottie asked.

"Just me." He set the sacks on the counter beside her. "I was supposed to have a bunch of siblings, but my parents were never able to conceive. My mom was forty-five and my dad was fifty when they found out they were going to have me."

"Wow."

He chuckled. "I believe that's exactly the word they used when the doctor gave them the news. They were thrilled to be parents, though they had to readjust their life. They said they felt a kinship to Abraham and Sarah in the Bible."

"What happened to them?"

That expression returned. It was a mixture of sadness and something else she couldn't place.

"They passed away about five years ago."

"I'm sorry."

He tucked his fingers into the pockets of his jeans and met her gaze. "Yeah, so am I."

She touched his arm briefly with a comfort she wished he could embrace.

"Though they were up in years, they were very active." He shook his head. "I never saw it coming. I thought they'd be here when I finally got ready to come home, but they were killed in a car crash. I still can't really believe it."

"What did you do?" Dottie gasped.

He lifted a shoulder. "After the funeral I went back to the city, but I wasn't seeing things like I had before. I was haunted by what had happened and by the things my dad had tried to show me." He paused, and shook his head. "It's odd, in the end it was Dad's death that sent his message home to me. Small towns need lawmen. They need well-trained response teams, and they needed to feel safe during emergencies. That can happen with the right training." He paused. "My dad had tried countless times to make me see that I was needed in Mule Hollow more than I was needed on the city streets. But I hadn't been able to see it. Didn't want to. Anyway, that's enough of that, long story short…I came home a little too late. But I came."

Dottie watched the smile that tugged at his lips and felt as if she'd known Brady Cannon all her life. He was a man of integrity and honor. And something was missing from his story. She could see it in his eyes, hear it in his tone.

It was also none of her business. He was helping her get ready for the fair, and to find out what he could about Cassie. She could admire the man. But she didn't need to dive headfirst into his personal life.

"We came here to make candy, didn't we?" he asked, efficiently changing the conversation for her.

"Yes, we did. Have you ever made candy before?"

He removed his hat, smiling. The smile showed off all his beautiful teeth and crinkled up the edges of his eyes.

"Nope, but I have eaten it before. How's about we make some more of those turtle cluster do-dads."

She laughed. "We will, but now that we have all this space I want to make peanut brittle. The do-dads will have to wait." They had two days left to cook and she planned to make the most of this kitchen.

"That'll do the job, too. I like brittle. I even have the marble tabletop my mom used to use to cool hers on."

"Get outta here! Do you really? That would be fantastic. I can cool it on cookie sheets, but it's not anywhere close to perfect like with marble."

"Follow me."

Dottie was glad to follow him. They went into the huge house with its wide halls and hardwood floors. It wasn't a showplace, but it was a welcoming older home that she could tell had been planned to be lived in.

In the front room, off the main hallway, was a spacious room decorated with antique furniture. Against the wall was a lovely marble table about one and a half feet wide and two feet long. Brady took the lamp off the tabletop, then easily lifted the heavy marble top from its resting place.

"My mom used to have Dad carry this to the kitchen table and there she'd roll out the brittle and let it harden. It's one of my fondest memories."

"Isn't that funny? Those memories of my grandmother and mother making candy are some of my warmest ones, too."

"Hey, Dottie," Cassie said, bursting into the room, pulling Jake behind her. "Look who I found wandering around outside."

"Hi, Dottie, Brady. I was passing by and Cassie had said y'all were going to be out here. Anyway, I was on my way out to the ranch, you know, to check on some calves, and wondered if—well, I was wondering if Cassie could go along."

"Do you mind?" Cassie asked, her eyes bright with

excitement.

Dottie's first inclination was to say yes she minded. But she couldn't. "No, go ahead, you got a bundle of stuff packaged earlier and I do appreciate that you did all that on your own." Dottie watched the younger woman blush and thought it was endearing.

"I enjoyed it. I used to work at this—" She stopped herself just as she always did with any information that linked to her life prior to Dottie picking her up off the roadside. "Anyway, I liked doing the packaging. And I can do some more later."

"Well, thanks, have fun." Dottie didn't know what else to tell Cassie. She wasn't exactly her keeper, though she did hope she had some influence.

"You're going to miss out on making peanut brittle," Brady offered in a voice of mock authority.

Dottie laughed. The man seemed to really be looking forward to making brittle. *You are, too. With him.*

The kids backed out the door. They didn't look at all worried about missing out on the candy-making experience.

"Why should I be surprised that they're passing up on this?" Brady asked.

"You didn't think they would actually accept your offer?" Was he pulling her leg again? He had a poker face when he wanted to. His dark eyes hid secrets in their depths.

"Actually, I think we can handle it all by ourselves." He was flirting with her. There was no mistaking the spark in his eyes with that statement. Dottie's heart leaped, remembering how it felt to be held in his arms. Spinning toward the counter, she started slinging open cabinet doors, looking, searching for, no not a bowl, not a measuring cup... Bingo, there was the ever-handy rolling pin! Just exactly what she needed to pound some sense into her ailing brain.

Sister, you know there is nothing whatsoever you would rather be doing than making candy with Brady Cannon.

She curled her fingers around the heavy piece of wood, and only then did some sense of sanity settle over her.

Anyone in their right brain would want to bake candy with Sheriff Brady Cannon. The man was a walking, talking billboard for chivalry. Why, she would be crazier by far if she didn't want to be spending time with him!

Okay, calm down. She took a deep breath and laid her weapon down. Relieved she hadn't taken a swing at herself, she turned back toward Mule Hollow's resident knight in shining armor. She was just going to have to deal in a mature manner with this immature infatuation.

That's what it was.

Banging herself in the head with cooking utensils certainly wasn't the answer.

Although, on second thought, it *could* put her out of her misery.

Dottie had just finished dressing on her third morning in Mule Hollow when the noise started. The sound was awful and had her running down the tiny hall in surprise just in time to see Cassie diving off her bunk, her eyes huge and questioning. They met in front of the door, huddled together in bewilderment. Dottie was certain the look on her face had to match the bafflement she saw on Cassie's.

When the noise erupted again they jumped and moved closer together. "What is that?" she whispered, not at all certain why she was whispering.

Cassie shook her head, her head of really bumpy bed hair.

"It sounds like a donkey!" Dottie lifted the curtain so they could peek out the window.

"It's Samantha!" Cassie squealed, jumping up and down laughing. "I can't believe it. Look at her."

"That's an elephant!" Dottie whispered, looking at the putty-colored rolls rippling down the little donkey's body. She was prancing around the trailer when suddenly she plopped onto her well-padded rump, reared her head heavenward, rolled back her lips and let out the most awful sound Dottie had ever heard. Or at least until a few moments earlier.

The awkward *e-haw* went on and on and on. "Let's go!" Cassie had swung the door open and jumped outside before Dottie could say no.

Not just no. But no, no, *no!*

She'd never been closer than maybe a hundred feet to a donkey and she hadn't been that close to many. She was usually passing them by in her car.

And that was the way she wanted it to stay. But as Cassie jogged across the grassy fifteen feet in her baggy shirt and shorts, Dottie followed at a slow amble. Afraid, but not feeling exactly right about letting Cassie go it alone to investigate the lumpy creature. Dottie was halfway to the bellowing burro when she saw the dog. It was a bedraggled fellow with long ears and a shaggy tail, and it was rolling in the dirt with its feet in the air and a silly grin on its droopy lips. It twisted its head in the dirt so that it could get a good look up at her and then it flopped over and jumped up, dirt falling from its coat like rain off a duck. Before she could do anything, the dirty dog lunged at her, hit her in the knees like a linebacker going for a tackle and sent her rolling to the ground.

Now, Dottie had many thoughts as she was being taken down by the hairy beast and none of them were nice. He was coming at her with his tongue dripping drool, when some Good Samaritan grabbed him and tugged him away.

"Lucky, no! We have got to work on your manners," Lilly scolded, her mop of dark hair bouncing as she tugged at the beast. "I'm so sorry, Dottie. Here, let me help you up."

Dottie laughed—*what else could she do?* And it was funny. Really, chickens the day before and a donkey and wild dog today. Tomorrow maybe it *would* be an elephant.

"Mule Hollow is never boring," she chuckled, taking Lilly's hand. If her hips weren't still stiff she'd have been able to get up unassisted. But her hips were a constant reminder of how far she had to go. Knowing Lilly was watching and wondering, it was aggravating to move like she was forced to. Still, thankful to be moving at all, she placed her hands on her knees before straightening.

"Are you okay?" Lilly asked.

"I'm fine. I just have an old injury. Nothing to worry

about. What are y'all doing down there?" She nodded toward the end of the field and the activity going on.

Lilly glanced away from her then. "Well, we're setting up the petting zoo. Samantha decided she wanted to go exploring. The ol' girl is a roamer by nature. And Lucky is a little overzealous at times. I'm really sorry. I think sometimes he thinks he's a bowling ball and we're the pins!"

"It's fine. Really. Honestly."

"Your back. Does it hurt?"

"Lilly. My back is good. It's the getting up and the getting down that I sometimes have a problem with. Samantha isn't going to bite Cassie or anything, is she?"

"No way!" Lilly gasped, reaching into her pocket. "That's why she's the main attraction at the petting zoo. Kids are going to love getting a ride on her back. All the money is going toward a new water truck for the fire department."

"That's a great cause."

"Yes, the truck we have is pretty ancient and we decided at the last town meeting that we would start doing something at each of these town-sponsored events to raise funds for a new truck. Of course, all the ranchers would kick in and buy it out of their own pockets, but we thought it wouldn't hurt to try and raise at least some of the money." Lilly scrunched her nose up and smiled. "Cort, my sweet sugar pie, thought of the petting zoo. Our son, Joshua, is a baby, but Cort loves children and thought it would be fun to give them a special place. And we're just asking for donations. The kids can ride for free if they can't afford a donation. Cort couldn't stand to let a child not enjoy the animals." Dottie smiled, glancing toward Lilly's husband, who, along with another cowboy, was manhandling the special gates that connected to make portable pens for the animals.

"He seems like a great guy."

"That's my man. Sometimes I have to pinch myself.... I guess I better round up Samantha and go help him before he starts to realize I'm letting him and Bob do all the work."

She pulled a piece of yellow candy from her pocket and called to Samantha. Cassie frowned at them when Samantha sniffed the air then immediately abandoned her, trotting toward Lilly. She was holding her hand out to the funny little burro and Dottie got tickled when Samantha batted her big brown eyes at Lilly, puckered her juicy lips and daintily nibbled the tiny square of what looked like yellow taffy from her flattened palm. "Samantha and I are fools for this stuff." Rubbing the burro between the eyes, Lilly looked at Dottie. "Come by and see us when you have a chance. We're going to have all kinds of animals."

"I'll do that."

Lilly turned to leave then spun back. "Hey, you're going to be here for a few days, right?"

"Ah, sure. As long as it takes to get my RV back up and running. I hope the mechanic comes home soon."

"You can't leave until you come out for supper."

Cassie walked up and caught the conversation. "You mean like a barbecue?"

"Sure. Would you like that?"

"Would I? Oh, yeah."

"Then that's what it'll be. See y'all later. Be sure and come see the petting zoo."

"She's nice," Cassie said as they walked back to the RV. "And those animals are hilarious. You know, Lucky used to be Loser."

"Do what?" Dottie asked.

"His name. It used to be Loser, but Lilly renamed him. Cort had given him his original name."

Dottie shook her head. "Leave it to a man to slap a name like that on a poor unsuspecting animal."

"Yeah," sighed Cassie. "My dog's name was Waldo." Dottie wasn't sure if Cassie realized she'd just given out information about herself. Not wanting to see her backtrack, she chose to say nothing. Every little piece of the puzzle would help her discover who Cassie was. The best scenario would be for Cassie to finally trust her enough to tell her about herself. But she was running out of time. If Brady didn't find out something soon then she was just going to have to chance spooking the girl by asking her some point-blank questions. "Are we going out to Sheriff Brady's place to finish the candy today?"

Brady. She'd tried not to think about what a blast they'd had making brittle. And that kitchen. If she had a kitchen that size and that layout in California, cooking class would be a dream.

"Earth to Dottie. Earth to Dottie."

Oh man, she had to stop daydreaming. Cassie was staring at her as if she'd been doing cartwheels and getting no recognition for the effort.

"Sorry. Brady said he'd be here to pick us up as soon as he came back from Ranger. He was going to drive over there first thing and check on Paul, the truck driver, at the hospital, and see how he was doing."

"He's so sweet. You two make a good couple. Kind of like me and Jake make a nice couple. Boy, I like him."

What was it with this town? Something was in the water and that was for certain. "Cassie, I know I'm just the person who gave you a ride to town—"

"And a place to stay," Cassie added with a crooked grin.

"True, but something tells me that there is an entire town that would give you a place to stay if you needed it."

"True, too," she agreed. "But I don't think I'd have my very own ritzy loft anywhere else."

"True, also. But I was going to say, I hope you, well, what I mean is—you said you came out here looking for a husband…and one minute it's Bob then Jake and you haven't even met Bob." She swallowed, glancing down toward the petting zoo and the cowboy Lilly had called Bob. She was glad for the moment Cassie hadn't heard that exchange.

"Dottie, don't worry about me. I'm *going* to find a husband. And Jake might be my man. He is so cute, and yesterday I got to pet a calf, and he showed me some that were being bottle-fed. I came out here for Bob, but a girl has to keep her options open."

Dottie sighed. "What would your mom say about you wanting to get married so young?" There, she'd said it. Just threw the question out there and took a chance.

"I don't need my mom's permission!" Her anger startled Dottie. "I'm *nineteen* years old! I'm my own person, Dottie. And I'm getting married. Do you realize that some people have lived enormous lives by the time they're nineteen? Enormous *happy* lives. I want to be a mother and a wife. Pronto! And I want to live in Mule Hollow with Lacy and Adela and Norma Sue and Esther Mae and all the rest of the lovely people who live here."

It hit Dottie that the girl had a point. One she herself was beginning to gravitate toward even after only two short days... Who *wouldn't* want to live in Mule Hollow?

CHAPTER EIGHT

Brady walked toward his house and could smell something sweet as he took the steps onto the wide porch two at a time. Memories of coming home as he grew up filtered across his mind. Tramping into the house as a boy, stealing cookies straight off the cookie sheet, his mother's laugh as she swatted at his hand.

But this was different, even though the scents and the welcoming light brought back childhood memories, this was very different. This felt like he was coming home to Dottie.

He stopped in his tracks. *What are you doing, Brady?*

Dottie was everything he'd ever wanted in a wife. She had a good heart, a strong faith and a nurturing spirit. She was beautiful inside and out...and she was leaving in a couple of days. It didn't make any sense to follow this attraction he felt for her. The best thing he could do was back off. Back off and let it go.

The laughter trickling through the door leading into the kitchen was like a slap in the face. It would have pleased his mother that there was life in her kitchen. She'd built this house to be lived in.

And he'd barely been existing in it.

"Hey, Brady," Cassie yelled as he stepped into the kitchen. "Thought you'd never get back. Get on in here and tell me what happened. I want all the juicy details." He hung his hat on the rack and ran a hand through his hair, which was damp with sweat from standing out in the sun trying to settle a dispute between two vendors. The vendors were arriving today to set up for the Trade Days opening tomorrow. And thus his job's headache had begun. But being out there was nothing compared to the headache of facing Dottie and the emotions he felt when she was near.

He focused instead on Cassie, and though he could feel Dottie's gaze he didn't look at her.

"Everything turned out fine. Red, the hot-dog man, got a tad hot under the collar because he was placed beside Harlen, the taco guy. As it turns out, they were beside each other at a fair up in San Angelo where Red had accused Harlen of unplugging his compressors so that all his hot dogs went bad."

"So, did they fight?" Cassie asked, an unabashed grin on her face. She hunkered down at the table and set her chin in her palm. "Who threw the first punch? Was it a good one?"

"Cassie!"

Dottie's exclamation drew his attention. She was smiling and his reflex was to smile back.

"Hey," Cassie declared. "So I like boxing, sue me. It's fun watching people act goofy. You know they know they're acting bad, so why not enjoy the show? They obviously like the attention."

Brady laughed. The kid had a point. Sort of. "Red threw the first punch." He shook his head when her eyes lit up and she let out a whoop. "Of course, Harlen immediately started yelling and that's when Ms. Belle stepped in. I got there just in the nick of time."

"Ms. Belle, who's that? And why'd she jump in there like that?"

"Cassie!" Dottie said again, laughing.

"She's the corn-on-a-stick lady. It seems many of these vendors hit the same circuit and these fellows both have their eye on Ms. Belle."

"Oh, a little competition."

"Hey, competition's a good thing, Dottie," Cassie said. "I'm gonna drum some up some myself— Oh, I hear Jake now. That boy can read my mind." She dropped the bag she'd been tying with a ribbon before Brady had distracted her. Hopping off her stool, she gave Dottie a quick hug then dashed out the door. Just as the screen door slammed, she suddenly twirled around, stuck her head back inside and grinned at him "Bye, Brady. Didn't mean to ignore ya! Oh, did you arrest them?"

He laughed. "No, I warned them."

"Good." Her expression of glee was comical. "Maybe there'll be some fighting tomorrow and I can watch."

And then she was gone, just like that—leaving him alone with Dottie.

"When she's done, she's done," he said, glancing at Dottie. She was looking especially nice today in jeans and a gold-colored shirt. She was concentrating on slicing a piece of fudge from the slab she'd made, so he concentrated on not focusing on her. Taking Cassie's vacated seat, he picked up the cellophane wrapper she'd been working on and tried to tie a bow. He needed to leave. To drop everything and walk out. Now.

"Have you heard anything?"

He looked up from his sad bow to meet her inquiring gaze. "Nothing. Someone should have missed her by now." It was true. He hated to say it, but if anyone cared about Cassie, someone would have reported her missing by now.

Dottie laid a hand across her heart, looking away out the window over the sink. But he saw the worry in her eyes.

"I—I know her dog's name is Waldo. She let it slip in conversation earlier. I think the more comfortable she gets, the more she'll tell. She might eventually confide in someone. Don't you think?" She turned back, hope in her expression.

Brady dropped the bag, giving up on the bow. It looked as if it had been run over by Jake's mud tires. "We need to talk to her. It's time."

She eased onto the stool across from him and studied his attempt at the bow, lost in thought. Then she nodded. "I'll talk to her tomorrow. She'll be okay."

He reached out and covered her hand before he could stop himself. This woman had been through so much and yet her heart was constantly thinking of helping others. When she lifted her eyes again to his, time stopped for a moment.

He swallowed. She took a small breath. And the clock over the stove ticked away the seconds.

How it happened he couldn't say. He leaned toward her and kissed her. When she answered the kiss it was like a gift.

One he couldn't accept.

Abruptly he stood and moved away. Leaving her dazed and wondering. Her eyes clouded.

"This can't work," he growled, like the animal he knew he'd just behaved like.

"You're right. It can't."

Her quiet answer wasn't exactly what he was expecting. He turned back to her and she was watching him. "I'm attracted to you," she said bluntly. "But I have a life waiting for me in L.A. and you have a life in this wonderful place. What you're doing here is admirable." Brady wasn't certain that he liked that she could kiss him the way she had, then calmly state all the reasons why this connection between them should be cut. It wasn't as if they were discussing light switches! But looking into her clear hazel eyes, sparking more amber than green, he knew that's exactly what she'd done.

There wasn't anything he could offer her. He didn't want or need romantic entanglements, so he should have been happy.

He wasn't.

Dottie had never been as glad to hear a vehicle drive away as she was now. The sound of Brady's engine faded and blended into the sounds of the night and she collapsed in the wicker chair in front of her RV.

Her nerves were shot. Shot! What had she been thinking? That kiss. Oh, that kiss.

It had taken her by surprise and the emotion that wrapped around her heart had scared her with its intensity.

No Place Like Home was waiting for her. Needed her. But in an instant... Oh, she was horrible, because in that moment, if Brady Cannon had shown the slightest inclination that he wanted what her crazy heart was wishing—she'd have abandoned her mission for a life with him.

How fickle was that?

Her name truly could be Dottie Marie Fickle Hart. It was no longer a joke! She'd been tempted to toss over everything the Lord had done for her. And everything she needed to do for Him. For the love of a man.

But that hadn't happened because Brady had made it extremely clear that he was married to his job.

Once they'd gotten over the initial shock of sharing the kiss, they'd gone about finishing up wrapping all the candy. They'd worked predominantly in strained silence, the ease that they'd shared gone.

Finally unable to take it any longer she'd started to talk. Expounding more fully than before about the miracle of her rescue. Thinking that if she could let him glimpse her heart it would make things easier between them. It also reminded her that she would have to come to her senses—that she shouldn't turn her back on her mission.

She knew this especially when she told Brady that she hadn't been alone down in that dark pit. God had been right there beside her. Even after her carelessness, He'd watched over her. It had been such an amazing, life-changing experience. Terrifying, but amazing. She'd heard of instances of devastation where survivors said they knew death was upon them and they gave in to it...then miraculously they'd survived. She'd told him how she'd felt the same, that instead of fighting she'd given over to the peace. To Jesus saying He was with her, that everything would be all right.

Dottie reached out and drummed her fingers on the patio table, watching the drooping flowers jiggle in the vase in its center. Brady had listened quietly, his beautiful brown eyes full of compassion.

Especially when she went on to tell him how she'd started reviewing her life leading up to the point that had led her to stay behind in the hurricane. That despite repeated warnings to evacuate her small coastal town, she'd been so determined to watch the storm. Foolishly, like there was anything she could have done to protect the home she'd inherited from her dear grandfather, who'd just passed away.

Her grandfather who'd urged her to step out and experience a full life. To take a risk. On further reflection, she didn't think he'd meant a risk so foolish. Dottie laughed even now, sitting under the stars thinking about her ninety-three-years-young granddaddy spouting off that when the Lord intended on taking him out of this world it would happen. That it didn't matter if he was climbing Mount Everest or sleeping in his bed or riding out a hurricane. That when his time on earth was done, he was outta here.

Brady had sympathized with her when she'd revealed that she'd figured out, while lying beneath the rubble, that she'd been trying to share an experience with her granddaddy by riding out a hurricane in his home. She'd been trying to hold on to him a little longer.

When they'd finally finished and he'd dropped her off at the RV, he'd grown quiet again, and she felt weary, sad and totally confused watching him drive away. She realized at this moment she wanted nothing more than to get this weekend over, have her RV fixed and get moving toward California.

It was time to get out of Mule Hollow. And away from the man who could very easily own her heart if she allowed it.

CHAPTER NINE

"**B**rady!"

Norma Sue. Brady groaned and slowed his pace. Friday, the first morning of the two-day event, had arrived way too early for him. He'd had a never ending sleepless night, he was tired and confused. His past had been nagging at him constantly after he'd dropped Dottie off at her RV. His heart was running away with him even as his head kept telling him that Dottie was leaving Mule Hollow and he didn't have any reason to think otherwise. To say the least, he wasn't in the best of moods. Norma Sue barreling down on him first thing made for a dangerous situation. It wasn't that he didn't like Norma, he did, but he wasn't the dullest guy on the block and he knew that the town had a hawk eye on him and Dottie. Due in part because of his stupid wink. He still hadn't figured out why he'd winked at her. Or kissed her.

"Brady Cannon, if I didn't know you better, I'd think you were trying to avoid me."

He sighed and spun on the heel of his boot to face Norma Sue. She hurtled to a halt in front of him. Her wiry gray hair was sticking out from under the cowboy hat she wore to protect her skin from the sun and her rounded figure was covered by a big denim work shirt and jeans. She'd come prepared for work today. His only hope was that that was what she wanted to see him about.

"Hey, Norma, I wasn't trying to avoid you, just had a lot on my mind."

She was sucking wind back into her lungs in deep gasping breaths. "I'm about to slap pass out. Whew-wee, getting these stubby legs to move fast enough to catch those long legs of yours is a trip and a half." Bending over, she placed her palms on her knees, shoulders heaving.

Feeling a mite alarmed, Brady bent down, too. "I'm really sorry, Norma. Can I help you?" He started patting her on the back but she waved him off, snatched her hat off her head and started fanning.

"Fine. I'm fine, just—" she held her free hand up "—give me a sec and another— Whew-wee, this heat wave we're having today hoodwinked me."

When she stood up at last, she was red faced, but grinning like the Mad Hatter. "I'm f-fine. I heard you been helping Dottie get ready for today."

Brady braced himself. The woman was on the verge of cardiac arrest and still her mind was one-track! But what had he expected? Everyone knew Norma Sue Jenkins had never been much for beating around the bush. "And who did you hear that from?"

"Actually, from Cassie. She was telling me a-walago that you were so sweet to have them out to cook at your place. Been wondering where they were during the day."

She was breathing more easily, and for that he was glad. He didn't want to start the proceedings with a call to the ambulance.

"It was the neighborly thing to do."

"Oh, yes, it was," she said, showing way too many teeth for his comfort.

"And *neighborly* is exactly what we want to be." She rammed him in the ribs! "You need a sweet girl like that, Brady Cannon. That girl has been here, what, four days? And she fits right in. And everybody can see that the two of you clicked right off."

He stepped away from her, rubbing his bruised ribs. "Norma, I don't want to interrupt your cakewalk or anything, but you can tell the ladies to back off." She was finding humor in this but it wasn't funny. Not that she could know that he'd started dreaming again. But this time the dream was of Dottie, dressed in black, crying at his graveside. It was a vivid dream fashioned from watching Eddie's wife weep her eyes out as she clung to the casket containing his partner's body. That was all it had taken for him to draw back. Dottie had a heart of gold and though the odds were low of him dying in the line of duty out here in the sticks, it didn't matter.

"Look, Norma, I let Dottie use Mom's kitchen and that's it. End of story. Y'all need to leave me out of this matchmaking stuff. I don't ever intend to marry."

"What did you say? Brady Cannon, you listen to me and you listen up good, son. I know losing your partner was hard on you. Don't look so surprised. Your mamma told me she thought his dying affected you more than you let any of us know. She was worried about you. And after your parents died and suddenly you came home…when you'd spent your entire life wanting to get out of Mule Hollow, we knew."

"Knew what?"

"We knew you needed time to heal. That your heart needed time to mend."

Brady started to deny everything she'd said, but she held up her hand.

"No need to deny it, son. You're a man. Men handle things different than women."

"Norma, you're steppin' over a boundary here." Brady bit the words out. He'd never talked to anyone about what happened—and he wasn't fixin' to start now. "Look, I've got to get to work."

"It'll all work out, son," she called after him. Brady kept on walking. He knew things didn't aways "work out."

Just ask Eddie's family.

The morning went from bad to worse.

It was like the vendors that had shown up were crazy or something. He decided right quick that he was going to have to talk to Lacy and the ladies about screening their sales force before future events, because by the middle of the day he was ready to throw in the towel and cry foul.

No way was he going to do this again.

If he hadn't known better, he'd have accused Adela and Esther Mae of putting something in the lemonade—everyone was acting peculiar! Not only had Red, the hot-dog man, and Harlen, the taco guy, finally duked it out over the corn-on-a-stick lady, the birdhouse lady and the free-puppy lady had almost gotten into a hair-pulling contest over the roasted-peanut man. And it only got better. There was the cotton-candy man and the flea-market collectibles lady... evidently they'd been an item along the route. Unfortunately, they'd picked Mule Hollow to decide to call it splitsville, loudly and obnoxiously in front of the dunk-a-dude booth.

Cassie was having a blast. Every time he looked up from a disruption, there she stood grinning like the show was all for her enjoyment. She was a funny gal. He'd finally been able to calm everyone down and despite wanting to haul the whole bunch to jail, he'd managed to control his temper and only hand out warnings. Only *after* making it perfectly clear that he had no problem changing his mind if they continued their behavior.

Cassie had not been happy with him spoiling her fun.

He was digging a bottle of ice water out of a chest when Dottie walked up. She wore a flowing summer dress the colors of the sunset, all reds and oranges with a splattering of gold, and she radiated warmth and happiness.

She took his breath away.

He hadn't thought he could say it, but he was glad he'd had so much keeping him busy. At least he'd had something to focus on other than the long line of cowboys who'd surrounded Dottie's RV all day long.

"You've been a busy boy this morning," she said, a gentle smile on her lips. "How are you holding up?" He ripped the cap off his bottle of water and took a long swig, an avoidance move on his part. "I'm hanging in there," he said, looking away from her. "Sorry I haven't made it over to your booth yet." He knew he could have. She did, too.

"Clearly I've been too quiet," she laughed, handing him a cute little package of assorted candy wrapped in a clear plastic wrapper with a glittering yellow ribbon. "I was thinking that you, above anyone else, needed a little care package. We've been watching you referee all day. It's been very entertaining. I'm sure you noticed how happy Cassie was. The girl was absolutely gleeful. Especially when it looked like the birdhouse lady was going to challenge you to a little wrestling match. She looked as if she might be able to take you, too."

"Thanks for the vote of confidence." He grinned and relaxed somewhat. Until he met her gaze. He took another quick swig of water and surveyed the field. It was safer than looking at Dottie with her shining black hair and sparkling eyes.

"There's a mass of people here," he said. Now they

were reduced to small talk. If things got any more strained they'd be talking about the weather next.

Dottie cleared her throat and gently kicked a weed with her sandaled foot. "For the most part they seem to be having a great time. Especially the kids. Do you see the crowd at the petting zoo? I think Cort was right about that. You may be able to purchase that equipment you all need very quickly."

"That would be nice. The people are great. It's these vendors I'm wondering about. For a while there I started looking for hidden cameras. I just knew I was on TV or something."

She chuckled, a gentle tinkle that drew his gaze to her again. And he realized he'd been waiting to hear it all day.

"Now, *that* would have been funny. Brady," she blurted his name out, then paused, as if she'd been waiting for the right moment to say what came next, but had to work up to finishing. "I wanted to say thanks for everything."

He met her gaze. A strand of long ebony hair drifted across her face and he had to fight the urge to reach for it, to tuck it behind her ear. "Already sold all of it?" He knew she had; cowboys weren't fools.

She laughed and visibly relaxed. "I've sold much more than anticipated. I had no idea that cowboys love candy so much! What a stampede we've had."

She was serious. She didn't get it. "They *like* the candy *lady.*"

Her gaze grew incredulous. "I hadn't thought of that. Cassie is really pretty, but honestly she wasn't at the table much."

"You know very well I was talking about you."

The crease appeared between her eyebrows and she cocked her head to the side. "Yeah, right." She yanked a thumb toward her booth and took a hesitant step backward toward it. "I guess I'd better get back over there... I just saw you having a peaceful moment and thought I'd come say hi and see if by chance any information pertaining to Cassie had come in."

"I hate it, but still nothing. If her name is really Cassie Bates, I'll know soon. But even if she's using a fake name, nothing with her description's turned up. You need to talk to her. Or I will if you'd like me to."

She shook her head. "I'll do it. You'd think she'd be starting to act like she was missing someone. But she's not. She's as happy as a clam. I mean, every day she gets happier. This morning she was bouncing all around, yapping like she does about cowboys and husbands. That girl has a one-track mind. She was talking about looking up Bob today."

"Oh, boy...and I thought things had calmed down."

CHAPTER TEN

"**D**ottie, you need to take a break and come with me. *Now.*"

She was in the middle of a sale and more customers were waiting in line. Brady's sudden reappearance and demand alarmed Dottie. "Is something wrong?"

"You could say that," he snapped, obviously not happy. Reaching for her arm, he helped her up from her chair, then informed the three cowboys in line holding sacks of candy that the sales were on him. They started to protest, but one glance from him and they decided now might not be the time to tangle with the sheriff. Especially since he immediately snatched her money bag and display basket, opened her RV's door, stuffed it all inside and led her away in all of a minute. "What's going on, Brady? Has something happened to Cassie?" Fear seized Dottie at the hard expression on his face.

"Remember that competition she was talking about? Well, she's drumming it up all right."

Weaving in and out of the crowd he practically carried her around groups who'd stopped to talk in the middle of the flow of traffic.

They'd gone all the way to the far end of the pasture when he stopped suddenly at the edge of a crowd. There was a lot of laughing and hooting as a young boy rode a mechanical bull. It moved up and down and around. It was obvious that the metal contraption could move much faster but was running at low speed for the child's sake. Dottie didn't understand what the big deal was. That is, until she saw Cassie standing beside the dark-headed cowboy in charge of the bull's controls. And Jake standing to the side looking forgotten about. His stance made it very apparent that he wasn't happy with the turn of events.

"Who is that?" Dottie asked, but by the look on Cassie's face she already knew. "Tell me that's not Bob."

"That's Bob, all right. And that's Jake. You may remember Jake, he's the one she's been flirting with— Ever. Since. She. Arrived. Here. He's the one wrapped around her pretty little finger."

Dottie groaned. "She said Bob was the reason she'd come to Mule Hollow. She said a lot of things. Is he looking for a wife? Poor Jake."

"Poor Bob." Brady tilted his hat back and grunted. "He wouldn't be averse to a wife, but I have a feeling he'd rather she be a bit closer to his own age."

"Has she been making a nuisance of herself? Or worse?"

"Just watch. She's ridden that bull about four times. Bob is having to give her pointers every time and then rescue her when she nearly falls off."

"She wouldn't."

"I'm afraid so. Here she goes."

The bull came to a halt and Bob picked the boy up and set him on the ground then turned to Cassie. Even from the distance where Dottie stood she could tell his smile was weak. He obviously didn't know what to do with the girl.

Ah, Cassie, what are you doing?

Dottie was embarrassed for the poor kid as she beamed up at him, oblivious to what was apparent to everyone else. The poor cowboy was being a polite gentleman and at the same time he was looking for an escape.

"What happened to the Jake infatuation?" she asked. "I mean, it's true, yesterday she was out there shaking hands with every cowboy she came within a hundred yards of. But she's been so into Jake."

"I don't know who she's trying to make jealous, but she did say she was going to get some competition going. I was talking to Bob when all of a sudden she zeroed in on him. Bob's a really nice guy, wouldn't hurt anyone's feelings, least of all a kid like Cassie. But..." His words trailed off as they watched Bob help Cassie hop onto the bull. He then proceeded to show her how to hold the reins. She was acting as if she hadn't a brain in her cute little manipulative head.

"Has he had to show her all of this every time?"

"Yup. 'Fraid so."

"Oh, Cassie. Cassie, Cassie. I'd never have thought she'd pull a scheme like this. I mean, she could have climbed onto that thing all by herself, she's smart as a whip and tough as nails."

Finished with the quick run-through, Bob stepped back and turned the bull on. Very slowly it started twisting and bucking. A two-year-old could have held on at the speed it was going. Cassie looked pretty good for a few seconds then the speed picked up to what any four-year-old could handle and she started calling for help! Clutching the saddle horn with a vise grip, she pretended to be slipping off the bull's back, looking imploringly at Bob.

Dottie could not believe her eyes. "Oh, give me a break! That is such a pathetic show of flirtatious bunk!"

"Tell me about it. This is my fifth time watching. I'd hoped she'd have moved on by the time I got you over here."

Dottie wanted to reach out and protect the girl from the foolishness. "Has she no pride?" she gasped when Cassie started slipping from the bull and cried out.

Brady grimaced. "Pride! Look at her."

Dottie was almost as relieved as Bob when Jake practically knocked him out of the way to get to be the hero. Apparently he'd taken all he could take. Scooping Cassie from her precarious perch, and despite her indignant protest, he strode past a much-relieved Bob to the outer edge of the gathering. All the while Cassie kicked her legs and glared up at the stone-faced young man who was on a mission to reclaim his status as her guy.

"Do you think we need to go over there?" Dottie asked Brady. Jake plopped Cassie down and the animated conversation began.

Even across the distance it was pretty evident that neither of them were happy.

"I think it'll be okay. Jake would never hurt her." Brady glanced down at her. "Maybe you could have a talk with Cassie pretty quick."

Dottie nodded just as Cassie shoved Jake and stormed away. Her face was red and Dottie wasn't certain, but she thought she'd glimpsed tears.

"I better go have it now."

Brady grabbed her arm. "Whoa, let her cool off. She might not need to know you witnessed all of that. And even if she knows, maybe she needs to have some time to reflect."

Torn with conflicting feelings, Dottie gave in. "You might be right. It's been a long day...a long week." Especially since she hadn't slept much. It had been hard trying not to think about Brady and the kiss they'd shared. And all the reasons she needed to forget about it. She didn't even know the man, really. Which was all the more reason this infatuation was disturbing her.

"Come on, let's take a breather," he said, breaking into her thoughts.

He took her hand and she let him tug her across the open field to a stand of low-slung trees. They were a scraggly lot with thin gnarled trunks, but they offered a nice quiet place to relax. That was the only reason she'd gone with him.

"I don't know about you," he said as they settled on the natural bench made by a double trunk of one of the gnarled trees, "but I feel like a dad going crazy over his daughter's dating choices. I'm worn smooth out. With all that I've contended with today, it's Cassie who has done me in."

Dottie crossed her arms and leaned back against the tree trunk. She fought to relax, to find a comfortable common ground with Brady. To ignore memories of the kiss they'd shared. "The poor girl is practically making a fool of herself over Bob. And in front of everyone. I thought my main problem was going to be convincing her to cut Jake a little slack. Man, oh man, was I ever wrong."

"She's a bit wet behind the ears, but I don't think she could have picked a safer place to mature."

Dottie sighed. "I know you're right. But I feel so responsible for her."

"God put her in your path for a reason. Do you believe that?"

Something in his voice changed with that question and she searched his expression. It occurred to her in that instant that God had put Brady in her path for a reason, too. Maybe it was to help Cassie out, but maybe there was another reason. She'd spent all this time with him, had seen him in action, knew that he gave freely to the community, to his job, but she really knew nothing more about him. Who was there for Brady?

What was his story?

"I do believe that God puts people in our paths for a reason. So why do you suppose our paths have crossed?"

She'd surprised him. So much so that he couldn't hide it. "To help Cassie," he said after a second.

"Maybe. I was just sitting here wondering what a great guy like you is doing without a family. What's your story, Brady Cannon?"

He cocked his head to the side and studied her. She smiled. "No joking? No winking? C'mon, what's your story?"

His expression hardened. "Let's see, Dottie with the good heart…you're out to save Cassie, you're on your way to help save a bunch of ladies in L.A. and now you think you can save me?" His gaze turned cynical. "It won't happen."

Dottie laughed, mostly from surprise. "That's the last thing I ever expected to hear you say." And it was. The good sheriff had changed, hardened right before her eyes.

"Why? Does that make me a bad person just because I don't want your help?"

"Nooo," she drawled through pursed lips. "But I see you out saving everyone around you, *Brady to the rescue,* and I can't help wondering, who rescues you?"

He stood abruptly and walked to the edge of the trees, clearly angry. The question was why? His reaction told her she was following the right lead. It felt similar to the moment she'd decided to pick up Cassie off the side of the road. Only, Brady hadn't had his thumb out.

"Let's just say I don't want to be rescued," he grunted.

"That's too easy."

He swung around. "What?"

She'd surprised him again. Rising, she walked to him. She wasn't sure what had come over her, but she was going with her gut. "You heard me, Brady. What's your story? I've wondered from the moment I met you why a great guy like you isn't married. It's none of my business, but if you want to talk, I'm here for you. It's the least I can do."

His expression told her he wasn't planning to take her up on her offer anytime soon. But that was okay. She'd said what she'd felt led to say. She patted his arm. "You think about it. You know where to find me if you want to talk."

She smiled at him then walked away. She should have felt bad about being so snoopy, but she didn't. She'd made an offer to someone she cared about and it felt good. Uh, cared about as a friend, of course.

Even if he didn't seem too fired up about the offer, it was out there. And now she needed to find Cassie.

CHAPTER ELEVN

Dottie found Cassie sitting on the backside of the RV in a chair she dragged there. It was a bit secluded and for that Dottie was thankful.

"Cassie, can we talk?"

The girl rubbed her eyes, looking down, then nodded. Dottie tried to pretend she didn't see the brightness left by the tears.

"I guess you heard."

"Actually, I saw." Dottie had decided to level with the girl.

"Oh."

"I've only known you for a few short days, but I get the impression that you could do just about anything you wanted to."

"Yeah, so what does that mean?"

Dottie didn't miss the return of the girl hitchhiker.

"So what was up with the bull riding? You and I both know that you could have ridden that thing standing on your head, at the speed Bob had it going."

Cassie rubbed the toe of her tennis shoe in the grass then looked up at Dottie. "Maybe."

"Maybe." Dottie couldn't help smiling. She really wanted to say the right thing. "What happened? Were you trying to make Jake jealous of Bob? Is that why you were pretending to be so helpless?" She prayed she didn't mess up.

"No, I wasn't trying to make him jealous. I had already realized when I saw Bob that he was the one I'd come to marry. I told you, reading about Bob in the articles made me know he was the man for me. I'm in love with him."

Dottie faltered at the revelation. "Those are strong words. What happened with Jake? I thought you were crazy about him."

"That's different. Like you said, he's a boy. Bob is a man. And a girl *needs* a man to marry, not a boy. That's what my mom needed! Besides, after the stunt Jake pulled, he can forget it. I'm done with him. Done. Did you see how he carried me off? I thought he was a really nice guy but that did it!" She jerked up out of her chair and started to walk away.

"Cassie—"

"I'll see you later, Dottie. I need to walk."

Dottie watched the girl hurry away and felt helpless. It seemed that everything was going downhill and she didn't know what to do about any of it.

"I'm tellin ya, I saw what I saw. Ole Applegate might be on the deaf side, but I ain't blind. With these here trifocals my eyesight's so good I kin still drive at night." Throwing his head back, he stared at Lacy through the large panes of his new glasses. Blinking, then adjusting them, he smirked at her like Barney Fife. "Yup, it ain't just everybody can say that thar. You jest ask that fool Stanley. He cain't see a lick come dark. Not a lick."

"Applegate, we're not saying you didn't see what you said you saw. I'm just saying maybe you need to keep it to yourself." Lacy could tell that App wasn't thrilled with that concept.

Why would he be? The man lived to tell all, but though she was cheering for a romance between the good sheriff and the lovely Miss Hart, she didn't want to be a part of idle gossip on their behalf. Staying clean of that stuff was hard, but she tried. "Look. Just because you saw them standing under the trees together doesn't mean anything. They could have just been resting in the shade."

"True enough," App grunted. "But I seen the way they eye each other when the other one isn't looking, and I'm telling you they were about to kiss."

Lacy sighed, staring at Applegate. She prayed for patience. She'd come to Sam's for a slice of pumpkin pie and a coffee. The day had been a success, brutally hectic but great, and now she was trying to wind down. When she'd first come to Mule Hollow she'd just known the women would come! And they were. Slowly but surely trickling in, renting houses that had long been vacated by families forced to leave years before when the oil wells dried up and work had to be found elsewhere. She'd seen many women come to know the Lord…there was nothing in the world more fun than sharing God's love with a person who didn't have a clue what they were missing out on.

But something was up. Something was brewing. She'd felt the Lord's plans for the tiny town were building toward something; she really didn't know what, though. Sure, lives were being changed and people were getting married, soon there would be babies… But she felt in her soul that there was more in store for Mule Hollow.

That there was a missing link somewhere. That the town was still waiting. Maybe that's what it was waiting for, the laughter of its first new generation of children. Whatever it was, she was certain they'd all know in due time.

"Lacy, just the gal I was looking for."

Lacy twisted around toward the door at the familiar voice.

"Hey, hey, Norma Sue, what's happening?"

Norma didn't smile or grin as she barreled her way past Applegate and slammed herself into the empty booth seat. That was Norma, always in a hurry. "Thank goodness you didn't put a nickel in the jukebox. I couldn't have taken hearing *Danke Schön* one more time, not that I hold anything against Wayne Newton. I'm tellin' you, when people find out that crazy box gets stuck on songs, they just go wild playing the thing into the ground. I thought Sam was going to have a nervous breakdown before I got *Great Balls of Fire* off there."

"Norma, Norma, Norma, what's got you in a tizzy?"

Norma took a deep breath and slowly expelled it. "It's Brady. What are we going to do? That boy has it bad. I can tell. You should see the way he looks when he's around, or even just talking about, Dottie. I feel it in my bones that she's the one for him, but he won't admit there's any connection. Did you know that Dottie is going to California to help open a women's shelter or something like that?"

"Yes. She's going to be the housemother and then teach the women business skills using the candy-making business as a model. I think it's wonderful. It's like when I came here. I was on my mission and now she's on hers. Isn't it cool?"

"Well, sure it is. But could you just fill me in on how that's going to help Brady? We can't have the boy moving away again. He just got back. And if the Lord has a place for Dottie in California then why'd He give her a layover in Mule Hollow? That's just cruel."

"Calm down, Norma Sue, it might not make sense to us, but the weird thing is it doesn't have to. Relax. It's gonna work out. I feel it in my heart."

Norma Sue heaved a heavy sigh. "I know you're right, Lacy. But for some reason this time it feels odd. It feels like we might be wrong. I don't know how, 'cause there's just too many things pointing to the two of them. You think we could be wrong?"

Lacy shook her head. "Let's just hang loose and see what happens."

Norma sighed. "Okay. It might be hard, but let's do that. And not a word out of you, Applegate Thornton," Norma snapped, shaking a finger at him. "I don't want to hear all over town tomorrow that our every breath is hanging on what the Lord has in store for Dottie and Brady."

Lacy coughed back a chuckle when Applegate

glared at Norma with a hard frown, not that his face wasn't in a perpetual state of *frownship,* but he emphasized it by clamping his lips tight.

"I don't know what gives you the idea I'd be talking 'bout Brady and Dottie. Just 'cause I saw them on a little rande-vu among the mesquite trees—"

"Applegate," Lacy said. "We've already been over that. They were probably just cooling off—"

Norma swung toward Lacy, excitement lighting her face. "They were under the mesquite trees? I didn't know they were under the trees together!"

"Norma!" Lacy exclaimed.

Norma slapped the table, looking repentant. "Sorry. But that could mean good things."

Applegate ambled past them, stopping at the door. "'At's why I ain't got any idea why you women think it's me spreading the gossip," he grumbled all the way out the door.

Lacy shook her head and then she and Norma Sue burst into laughter.

"You have to love the ol' fella," Lacy laughed.

Norma shook her head. "Says who?" Lacy raised an eyebrow.

Norma scowled. "Okay. But just a little."

Dottie's hip throbbed, her head hurt and she had never

been so glad for a day to be over in her entire life. How long could days be? How much could happen in one day?

More than she could take.

As eventful as the day had been, Dottie thought she would have slept like a log, but she hadn't been able to sleep a wink. Now, Cassie, on the other hand, was snoring like a train. Obviously worn smooth out from chasing poor Bob around all afternoon. Here she'd thought Cassie had gone off to lick her wounds when she'd stormed away. Instead, she'd headed down to the petting zoo to follow Bob around while he helped out with the animals and the kids.

Taking a deep breath, she rested her head against the back of the wicker chair, staring up at the midnight sky. The soft sounds of laughter drifted across the night air, other vendors winding down from a long day.

She closed her eyes and thanked the Lord once more for the gift of life. For the opportunity she had to make a difference in California. And she prayed that for Cassie and Brady. And she prayed for sleep... restful sleep.

She needed it...

CHAPTER TWELVE

The next afternoon Dottie took a deep breath then knocked lightly on the thick wooden door. Like the rest of Mule Hollow, the sheriff's office had been painted a bright color, but it was an understated chocolate brown trimmed in deep ruby.

"Door's open," Brady called from inside.

Her pulse fluttered at the sound of his voice and she had to force herself to twist the knob and peek around the door's edge. Despite her efforts, she'd found herself watching him all morning. From a distance. It wasn't as if he'd made any attempt to come anywhere near her. No doubt thinking he would be forced to endure some of her free-flowing advice of yesterday. And did she blame him?

"Do you have a moment?"

"Sure," he said, jerking to his full height, obviously

surprised to see her. He was around his desk in a flash, pulling open the door she was clutching with a death grip. "Come in."

She swallowed hard, and concentrated on Cassie, not the fact that she was really glad to be standing so close to him. This was about Cassie. The kid she'd brought to town to stake her claim on poor unsuspecting cowboy Bob.

He couldn't get away from the girl. After having been followed by Cassie all weekend, the poor guy was looking so flustered that Dottie had decided it was time to consult with Brady.

Rubbing her palms on the fronts of her jeans, she took a soothing breath and stepped into the office. The click of the door made the butterflies burst into rapid flight in the pit of her stomach. "I've come about Cassie," she said quickly.

"I'm still checking. Sit down." He held the old leather chair for her then leaned against his desk and crossed his booted ankles. "Did you talk to her?"

"Well, I tried."

"You tried." His eyebrow lifted and his chin angled. Dottie quickly told him about their conversation, feeling woefully inadequate.

"Did you press her about her past?" he asked when she'd finished.

"She didn't give me the chance." A knock on the door sounded and then Bob himself stepped into the room.

"Brady, I need to talk." His surprise at seeing her was written on his face. "Oh, hi, Dottie. Sorry, have I interrupted something?"

Shaking her head, she glanced at Brady.

"Come in," he said. "What can I do for you?"

"Well, since you're here, too, Dottie, I think it'd be okay to say this to both of you. I don't know what to do about Cassie. What's going on with the kid? I'm assuming you know what I'm talking about?"

They nodded. He kept right on talking. Fast.

"Any ideas for me? Or Jake? Or Cassie? I know you picked her up on the side of the road, Dottie…do you think she's in some kind of trouble? She's, well, she's trying too hard and I'm confused as to why all of a sudden she's hanging on me. Honestly, I never thought I'd say it didn't feel right to have a pretty woman hanging on my arm…but this just doesn't feel right."

Dottie looked at Brady, who'd moved back to his seat behind his desk. She nodded.

"I think it's safe to tell you, Bob, that we do have our questions about Cassie. We're not sure how old she is or anything else about her. But we're looking out for her and actually we were meeting to discuss the issue.

We don't want to do anything to upset her, and right now she's a little agitated. We don't want her bolting again if it does turn out that she's a runaway."

Bob's eyes clouded and he hung his head. "Man, that's tough, for the kid."

"Bob," Dottie said, "I'm sorry about what she did yesterday. There was something about the desperation in her actions yesterday that has me really worried that there may be something more going on below the surface. Brady tells me you are a great guy with a lot of integrity. Do you think that maybe you could just, well, could you be patient with her for a little while? Watch out for her, in a way. I'm not saying lead her on or anything, just try not to say anything that would cause her to become embarrassed by her actions and want to leave Mule Hollow."

To Bob's credit, Dottie saw compassion in his eyes. "I can do that. I'll do whatever it takes. She's a sweet kid. I like her. It would be a shame to see her hurt."

It was easy to figure out why Cassie thought she was in love with Bob. No wonder Molly had written several stories featuring him. He was wonderful. And not simply because of his dark curls and deep dimples. Tipping his hat to Dottie, Bob left them alone again.

Dottie turned back to see Brady studying her and felt a catch in her heart.

"You were all set to talk to her, and now you want to go slow again. What haven't you told me?"

"She started to make a statement about her mother. I'm thinking part of this infatuation with Bob has something to do with bad choices made by her mom. She's hurting. I know it. And so I revisited my rash case of big mouth and decided that caution might have merit."

"So you're telling me that you aren't going to be there for me when I decide to open up?"

She deserved his sarcasm. Really, she had been so smug. Who was she to think she had any answers?

"Look, I know I stuck my foot in it yesterday and said some stupid things. Who am I to say you have something bugging you? Just forget I said anything and let's concentrate on Cassie." Their gazes met and for the longest moment they just stood there and studied each other.

"Anyone invite the two of you to church tomorrow?" he asked finally, pretending that nothing was passing between them.

"Are you kidding!" Two could play this charade. "About twenty people."

He laughed, but his beautiful coffee-colored eyes didn't sparkle. "That's my town."

"Yes, it is. I'm coming and I'm going to try and talk

Cassie into joining me. As she put it, she and the God stuff don't get along. Of course, she said that in front of Adela and Lacy and a few of the other ladies."

"Oh, brother! Did she know she'd just made the challenge of a lifetime?"

"She didn't. I, however, saw every ear within earshot perk up. I knew she was among friends who cared enough about her to take it upon themselves to try and show her how much God loves her."

Brady nodded, a solemn expression settling over him. "Mule Hollow is a great place for injured souls, Adela and the others will mother her to death. She'll be okay."

Dottie thought about that, though she'd only been here a few days, he was right. Mule Hollow was special.

Lunch at Lilly's was a warm and lively experience. Church had been an experience; never had Dottie seen so many singing cowboys. Why, her grandma Sylvia, who was a huge Allen Jackson fan, would have thought she'd entered Heaven's Gates seeing so many long tall cowboys spiffed up and harmonizing. That included ultra good-looking bachelor Bob, which was Norma Sue's incentive to get Cassie to go to church with them.

Now Cassie sat at the end of the table with Lilly, playing with baby Joshua. It was nice to see her involved in something other than man hunting. She looked happy.

As lunch progressed the conversation turned quickly to her work in California.

"So you're going to open up a candy store?" Norma Sue asked, carrying a fresh apple pie to the table, and swatting her husband, Roy Don's, hand as he reached for the knife.

Everyone seemed extremely interested in Lynn, Rose, Niva and Stacy. Not to mention the four children. Dottie could talk endlessly about the women. Each had a hard history and she was thrilled with how God was working in each of their lives.

"Yes, it's what I know. And after I got down there to test the idea out I was thrilled to see the eagerness everyone showed to learn the trade."

"You think there's a good market for something like that?" Esther Mae asked. She was sitting beside Dottie and had leaned near to whisper it in Dottie's ear. The big blue feather sticking off her hat batted Dottie across the eyes.

She shifted out of the way. "Sure I do," she replied quietly, not certain why they were whispering.

"What you whispering about over there, Esther?"

Norma Sue demanded, slapping a hunk of pie on Roy Don's plate. "Don't you know it's bad manners whispering at the table. Especially when you know I hate secrets."

Esther Mae threw her head back and harrumphed. Her big blue feather did a little jig and a plume of blue fuzzies drifted over Dottie. She sneezed.

"God bless you, child," Esther Mae chirped. "Hope you aren't catching a cold! I'm not telling a secret, Norma."

"Then spit it out."

"Norma Sue Jenkins. You are about the nosiest—"

"Spit it!"

"For cryin' out loud, Norma! I just asked if Dottie thought the candy business was a good business."

"Well, of all the silly questions. Didn't you see how fast she sold out of that black gold of hers? Everyone wanted some of that fudge."

Dottie waved away the fluttering fuzzies and fought off another sneeze. "I got an e-mail this morning from Stacy." Esther Mae swung back toward her, feather and all.

"That's the quiet girl, isn't it?"

"Yes." Dottie was pleased that she remembered. "She's had a terrible life and she doesn't talk much.

The entire time I was there, I only saw her smile a few times. And that was at her baby." Dottie thought about the personal history her brother had shared with her about the young woman. Stacy lived in a compartmentalized world with just one door. A door that she kept firmly closed to most of the world. It was a learned trait, since she'd lived to survive the abuse of, first, her father and later, the husband she'd married to escape the father. For Stacy, life had been a continual ride of hurt until the day she'd met Rose while washing clothes at a washateria. Rose shared her newfound faith with Stacy and it had changed her life.

Dottie still fought tears thinking about the e-mail from Stacy. Though she didn't feel it her right to share Stacy's personal past with everyone, she felt compelled to share how Mule Hollow and the wonderful residents had touched her life.

"So what did she say?" Norma Sue asked, shoveling a piece of pie onto Brady's plate.

"Stacy wanted to know all about Mule Hollow. She's even gone online and found every article that Molly's written about this town. She's so captivated by you. She wants to know everything there is to know."

"I just want to bring her here right now!" Lacy exclaimed. Like everyone else, Lacy had been listening intently. Now she leaned forward, placed her elbows on the table and demanded that Dottie tell her more about her plans.

Dottie smiled at the expectant crowd sitting around the table, including Brady. He hadn't said much to her all afternoon, but she'd caught him watching her often as he conversed with the guys.

There was just a tension around them that neither could deny. Though they may have said that kiss they'd shared didn't matter…it did. They'd been skirting attraction between them for days. And in silent agreement they would likely continue to avoid it.

She still didn't know what was bothering Brady, but something was. And it was making him distance himself from her on a personal level with every moment that passed. For Dottie, all it took was having a conversation about Stacy and the others at No Place Like Home to remind her of why she would keep pretending that that fluttering sensation hadn't taken up permanent residence in her solar plexus.

She knew her reasons, understood them, but meeting his gaze across the table, she couldn't help being curious as to what kept him from perusing any relationship. She shouldn't be thinking about it. She was leaving. But looking at him, she couldn't help it.

There was something about Sheriff Brady Cannon that she found almost irresistible. Not any one something…it was the entire package. He was devastatingly handsome, unerringly faithful to his job and the people under his watch and yet he was alone. Thoughts of him wandering around inside that gigantic house of his all alone brought tears to her eyes and she couldn't explain it. Who was supposed to break through that wall—that wall that it seemed only she could see.

CHAPTER THIRTEEN

They were getting ready to head home when Jake showed up. He stepped down from the seat of his huge truck and Dottie had to smile. The dude was, as Cassie would have said, hunky! Hey, if she were ten years younger, Dottie would have said it, too. He wore a pair of knee-length swim trunks, flip-flops, a T-shirt with the arms cut off and a cowboy hat that had the rim curled up on the sides and bent non-traditionally down in the front and back like the younger cowboys had started wearing them. He looked as if he was ready to have some serious fun.

And he'd come for Cassie.

She snubbed him at first, but Dottie could tell she was interested and trying hard not to show it. The boy was her age. Jake was off the Richter scale for cuteness. He was ready to have a good time and he wanted to share it with her. *Those things had to matter.* Dottie was glad Cassie had already changed into jeans, so she had no excuses.

"Cassie," he said, "if you stay behind, you're going to miss out. We've got an acre wet down and everybody's coming."

"Is Bob?" she asked flippantly.

Dottie could have wrung her neck. But Jake took it like a man.

"*I'm* going to be there," he said with more force than Dottie had expected. "And *I'm* the only one that counts."

To Dottie's surprise, Cassie stuck her hand in her back pocket, and smiled shyly up at the earnest cowboy. A few minutes later when she rode away in Jake's truck, Dottie felt a great sense of relief. Not that she was hoping they'd fall in love anytime soon. But they did seem to be right for each other. Maybe at a later date, though.

"You're smiling like that went well."

Brady walked up to stand beside her. His arm was touching her shoulder, her pulse jumped immediately. "It did actually. They're going mudding. It sounds like fun."

"You want to go?"

She didn't know what she'd expected, but it certainly wasn't an offer of an afternoon of fun.

"Really?" She knew she was gaping. She knew she should be saying capital N-O.

"Yeah, I go out sometimes and take my ATV."

"ATV?"

"All-terrain vehicle. Or four-wheeler, as we rednecks call it."

The corners of his lips turned up into that adorable Brady grin, a tinge crooked on the edge. Dottie's mouth went dry.

"Oh—" She swallowed the cotton. "I've never been mudding before. But...I don't want to get in Cassie's way. I don't want her to think I'm following her."

"Then we'll go on our own mudding expedition. I've got the perfect spot on my place. We'll go easy. I don't want to harm your back."

It sounded fun, though she was curious as to why all of a sudden he was inviting her, when he'd spent so much time avoiding her. *Just say no!* her sane side yelled. "Okay."

"Okay," he echoed, suddenly looking as uncertain as she felt. "First I think we'd better go back and let you change into something more appropriate than that dress."

"You don't think this'll work?" She looked up at him in mock shock, swishing the fluttery skirt. *Are you flirting with him?*

He scanned the dress and shook his head.

161

A pebble skidded across her stomach and she took a deep breath. She was leaving tomorrow or the day after that and she was suddenly feeling reckless. "Then I guess I need to put on some jeans."

He swung away and headed toward his truck. "That would be better."

Climbing into the truck, Dottie felt self-conscious seeing the smug looks on Norma Sue's and Esther Mae's faces. Even Adela was smiling and Lacy gave them a thumbs-up as she wrapped her arm around Clint's waist.

This was not good, giving them false hope that their matchmaking wishes had a chance. But at the moment, fun just seemed more important. She ignored her guilt and glanced at Brady.

By the look on his face, he was having as many second thoughts about the situation as she was.

She told herself to ignore the disappointment his frown caused her. But there were some things a woman couldn't ignore.

Brady hadn't considered when he'd made his rash offer of a mudding excursion that she would have to hold on to him on their ride. He still hadn't figured out what had possessed him to make the offer. Especially since he'd been trying to distance himself from her ever since they'd kissed.

But she was leaving and he enjoyed her company. So he told himself it wouldn't hurt anything for him to relax and enjoy her company while she was here.

He hadn't counted on the feel of her arms around him. Or the rightness of the sound of her voice in his ears and the thrill her laughter gave him.

He was flirting with fire.

He knew it. But he also knew that for now he was going to enjoy every minute of her company.

The sun was going down as they topped the hill overlooking a low land he called "the bottom" because of the way it flooded when the river was up.

"I love this area," he said, pulling the ATV to a halt.

Dottie flexed her fingers against his stomach, as if not sure if she was supposed to continue holding on to him now that they'd stopped moving. He placed his hand over hers, letting her know that her wonderful hands were exactly where they belonged.

Looking down, he smiled. Her hands were small— long slender fingers tipped with short nails. He loved the way they felt beneath his. He'd watched her mixing batter with those hands and had imagined how they would feel holding his. Now that he knew, it was going to be tough to let them go. But he would. For her own good. She deserved security.

"What is this place?" she asked, having to lean forward because he'd held her arms in place against him. Her breath feathered against his cheek.

"This is my favorite spot. The river cuts through here and it's beautiful. The mud down below is left over from when the river overflows."

"Can we get closer?"

He glanced over his shoulder. It was a dangerous move on his part because it brought their faces closer. So close that her hazel eyes took his breath away and the feel of her breath against his cheek was unlike anything he'd ever experienced.

"You can see it. But I'm warning you, not many people have ever been allowed back here," he teased.

"Really? Does that mean you'll have to kill me once I've seen it?"

There was the gentle tinkle of laughter he'd come to…look forward to. "Naah, you're special. I'll let you live. And come back here as much as you want. As long as it's with me." *Why did you say that, Brady?*

Her fingers moved beneath his, and her gaze slid away. He understood immediately that he'd made her uncomfortable. He'd made *himself* uncomfortable.

"Hang on." He revved the motor and took them down the steep embankment; she gasped and clung to him more tightly as the ATV crept down the craggy hill. When they'd made it to the trees, he took the trail he'd traveled all of his life.

"This is the place I used to come with my dad." He stopped at the edge of the river. "We'd come here after working cattle all day and relax in the cool water before heading home. Those were the days."

Dottie chuckled. "You sound so old."

He turned to look at her again and they bumped noses.

"Hey." She pulled a hand free and rubbed the end of her nose. He laughed watching her, knowing she was nervous, wanting so much to kiss her. Even with the mud clinging to her cheeks.

Wanting so much for this moment to last forever. But with nothing to offer her, it was wrong.

Dottie's laughter died in her throat. She'd been running on nervous energy the entire ride through the mud, and now that they were stopped she couldn't deny all the nerves were a direct result of her proximity to Brady. His smile sealed the deal. This was not fair.

"Well, are you going to show me more?" she asked,

needing to break the moment. To breathe.

His eyes sparked mischievously. "Hold on. This could get crazy and I wouldn't want to lose you."

For a woman who'd been almost crippled only seven months earlier she could not have fathomed the exhilarating freedom riding through the weeds and the dirt with Brady gave her. They flew like the wind along the bank of the river and when they reached a rocky area, Brady pulled to a stop beside a large rock that overlooked a section of raging water. It was breathtaking. Before she knew what he was up to, he stepped from the ATV up onto the flat rock. It was such a smooth move she knew he'd done it many times before. When he turned back and held out his hand, she took it immediately.

Once she was beside him, she turned away from him to stare across the water. Her heart was pounding and her thoughts were colliding more than the river churning down the rocky path.

"So I'm guessing you and your father never swam here?" Her breath was shallow as she asked the question.

"You'd be right about that."

She heard the smile in his voice even though she didn't turn to see his face. He knew exactly how she was feeling and he also knew that she was using diversionary tactics.

"Do you want to sit and relax for a while?"

His question was a whisper against her ear. She shivered but nodded. He startled her when he suddenly jumped the four feet to the ground and whipped around to look up at her. Before she could stop him, he took her by the waist and lifted her down to sit on the rock in front of him.

Everything went still. He studied her face. Searched her eyes. And Dottie couldn't breathe. It was as if the beautiful setting swirling around her was sucking all the oxygen from the air. She prayed a fervent prayer; she prayed God would take pity on her and give her a clue as to what was happening. She had a plan. She knew her path. She knew all of this, but right here in the midst of the beauty of the land and the warmth of Brady's friendship she could picture another life's path. She could see life with Brady. Children, family, a love so full that her heart was bursting inside the confines of her ribs. Suddenly he turned and stepped away from her.

She breathed in a sigh of relief and clasped her hands together. *Focus, Dottie. Focus.* Remember, he said when they'd kissed that it wouldn't work. He said he would never marry. He'd been distancing himself from her…until now.

Why had he asked her to come here? Why had she accepted? To learn more about him?

"Tell me about coming here with your dad. And about leaving Mule Hollow. You said your parents hadn't wanted you to go."

"Well…" He glanced at her then turned toward the water. "I left all of this right after I graduated. I couldn't wait to see the world. The world being anyplace but here." He shrugged. "I got accepted to the academy, after college at Sam Houston down in Huntsville. After school I took a job in Houston and thought my dreams had come true."

Dottie smiled when he ducked his head and looked over at her. He leaned against the rock beside her and crossed his arms over his chest. He was confident and at ease. It was a very appealing sight.

"But something happened, didn't it?" She couldn't help it. She was curious about him and suddenly she wanted to know why he didn't want a family. It had something to do with his past. It had to. A man didn't just decide not to have a family for no reason. Besides, she'd seen the hurt in his eyes.

He glanced her way and she saw his impulse to close the door again.

"Please tell me. I know I was all arrogant that day in the mesquite trees. But I really am here to talk."

He nodded, she could almost see his decision to trust her. It caused a feeling she couldn't quite place to pulse through her. But she liked it. It linked them together. "Like I told you the other day, my parents hated that I wanted to leave Mule Hollow. My dad kept telling me the town needed a man who wanted to be an officer. Sheriff Newman had been the sheriff here all of my life. I think he'd held the office unopposed for, like, fifty years. When he finally retired, the town had no one. Not that there was a huge need at the time. But, believe it or not, every once in a while they do need emergency personnel."

"I believe it. I mean, I was there…the small town where I'm from is not much bigger than Mule Hollow."

"The men who saved you were dedicated. Were they trained well?"

It was a question. Dottie nodded. "Yes. They took their emergency skills very seriously. They each knew what they were supposed to do. They'd mapped out their disaster procedures and worked according to plan. Two were right beside me, but it took a collaborative town effort to pull me from the rubble. But what happened to you?"

For a moment she thought he would deny understanding what she was asking. Then he nodded.

"I could tell you that I couldn't cut it. That the city didn't agree with me, that I couldn't cope with…but it would be a lie." He paused, studying the ground. "Actually, I was very good at my job. I was about to make detective when—" He raked his hand through his hair and Dottie reacted by reaching out and touching his shoulder.

"You know I told you my parents died in a car crash." He paused. "Well, about a month before it happened, my partner was fatally shot in the line of duty."

Dottie gasped. "Oh, Brady. I'm so sorry."

"Yeah. So am I." His eyes were so terribly sad when he looked at her. "He had a wife and kids. The twins were four. Just babies." His broad shoulders slumped. "Babies." She heard the anger then.

Her heart ached for the young family torn apart by a violent world and for Brady. She studied his profile and suddenly urgently wanted to comfort him.

"I'd never considered what happened to a family when a husband or parent died in the line of duty. I don't know, until I walked in and saw them so torn up I'd naively believed watching Eddie die was the worst thing that could happen."

She understood, at least in part. He didn't want to

leave anyone behind. He'd been hurt deeply.

"My mom and dad knew I was messed up. Dad had tried to talk me into coming home. At least for a visit, he said, to see how much Mule Hollow needed me. But I wouldn't."

Dottie couldn't stop herself. She laid her hand along his cheek but didn't speak. There was nothing to say. Just being here was the important thing.

"When I did come home—for the funeral—I saw what my dad had tried to tell me. There was a need. But I came home to forget as much as to help." He looked at her. "That doesn't sound noble, does it? Now you know I'm selfish."

"You sound human to me."

He shifted to face her, searching her eyes. Gently as a feather he touched her cheek and her breath caught in her chest. "I don't think I'll ever marry."

A picture of Brady growing old alone flashed across her mind. "I don't understand. You would be a wonderful father. The house is—"

"I chose to be a cop. I believe it would be unfair to father children when I could walk out the door one morning and not come home at the end of the day."

"But Brady, it happens every day. As callous as it sounds, all parents die sooner or later. That's how life is. Those of us left behind…we cope. We go on."

Taking her hand, he studied it then placed a gentle kiss inside the palm.

"Not on my watch."

"But that's crazy, Brady!" she exclaimed, surprised by the violence of her rejection of that thought.

"Why? People choose careers over family every day. It would be abusive and selfish for me to bring kids into this world knowing my job is dangerous…. Yeah, I know I'm the sheriff of a two-bit town. But it only takes one bad call. One slipup, and my family would be left behind."

"But Brady, cops have to have lives, too." This was insane.

"It's not just the threat of being killed on the job, it's also that the divorce rate is high. I saw it." He raked a hand down his face. "Dottie, this conversation is moot. I don't know why I even brought you out here today."

"Maybe you just needed someone to talk some sense into you."

Their eyes met, his were defiant and she knew hers were their equal. The level of emotion ran high between them, the sound of the rushing water behind him seemed to match the pace of the blood pounding through her veins. Filling her senses.

His gaze dropped to her lips.

"No, I brought you out here to have fun. But this attraction—" He backed away, meeting her eyes. "Look, I realized finally you need to understand why nothing can come of this. I thought you needed to understand."

She lifted her chin, her gaze connecting with his more fully. "Well, I don't."

CHAPTER FOURTEEN

Dottie stared at the night sky and fought the tears. Life was just not fair.

Brady had ended their afternoon with as much tension between them as they'd started out with. The man was stubborn to a fault. Hardheaded as any man she'd ever met and narrow-sighted when it came to changing his mind on family.

Cassie had left her a note that she was spending the night at Lacy's place to help deliver a calf. So Dottie was alone.

Feeling suddenly lonesome, Dottie decided to reach out to life at the end of the computer keys by writing Todd about her strange and overwhelming feelings for Brady.

However, when she turned her computer on, an e-mail from Todd was waiting for her.

His news was unexpected. The worst of her fears had happened. The powers that be had come to an agreement early and in one sweep of a pen No Place Like Home had lost its lease. They were to move out immediately.

Ten days.

How had this happened? She understood that God hadn't said life would be easy. But she didn't understand why sometimes there never seemed to be a break in the clouds for some people.

Needing to seek God's guidance, Dottie started walking and praying. Her hip throbbed a little from the afternoon ride, but it couldn't compare to the pain in her heart.

Lord, Lord. I don't understand....

She thought she was just wandering, lost in prayer, until she found herself in front of the beautiful older home at the end of Main Street that belonged to Adela Ledbetter.

Dottie had come to know Adela as a lovely woman of strong faith. Dottie needed to talk to someone, so without hesitation she walked up the pathway. Her heart was heavy, her emotions frayed. When Adela answered her knock a tear rolled down Dottie's cheek. "Oh, dear, you look like you could use a friend and a hot cup of tea."

There were times in her life that Dottie knew God had placed specific people in her path for specific reasons. Looking into the startlingly wise eyes of Adela, she knew this was one of those times.

"Thank you, I really need a friend right now. A Godly friend."

Adela took her arm and led her over the threshold and into her beautifully crafted historic home. It was like stepping back in time, with the wide entrance hall, intricately carved stairway and elaborate antique furniture.

"Now come into my kitchen. Sit. Relax while I make tea and then you tell me what has you so upset."

Dottie took the chair offered, cupped her hands on the table and watched the petite woman fill the teakettle with water.

"I've been praying for you," she said, glancing over her shoulder at Dottie.

The simple words washed over Dottie. "You have?" Adela nodded then reached for the tea bags. "The moment you arrived in our delightful town, God placed you on my heart. The story of your survival, your faithfulness, you've been through the fire and lived. It's amazing. Really. You have a special purpose."

Dottie closed her eyes and took a deep breath. She had been through the fire. "God's been good to me."

And He had, so how could she be so angry at Him. Because she realized that was exactly how she felt.

After a moment Adela brought the tea in two dainty china cups to the table. "Now, dear, what's upset you?" Dottie managed to tell Adela about the home losing its lease. "I just don't understand, Adela. These women were doing so well. They were making progress. I don't understand the heartlessness of the landlords doing this. But I especially don't understand God allowing it. I mean He placed Stacy and Rose on my heart. He's given me this opportunity—or so I thought—to be used by Him, and now it's gone. What will they do?" Adela watched calmly with her wise eyes. "They will do what they will do. It's that simple. What will *you* do?"

Dottie paused. "Excuse me?"

Adela took a sip of tea. "Will you pray? Will you give up because the plan hasn't progressed as you've seen it in your heart? What will you do?"

Good question. "I don't know, Adela. When I read that e-mail I was so upset because I thought I clearly saw God's plans for me. I mean, all those months in the hospital I prayed for Him to give me a reason to understand why this had happened to me. You see, for a while I'd been feeling like there had to be something more to life than just getting up and going to work every day and making money." Dottie took a sip of her tea, savoring the touch of lemon. "Then, like an answer straight from God's heart, Todd suggested I would be good for the ladies at the women's home he'd started a few months back. He had no idea of my feelings when he said God had placed it on his heart that maybe I might be ready to use my business skills as a mission opportunity."

Adela smiled. "That's how He works. He prepares the way even before we see the path."

"Yes! I've believed that with all my heart. And that's why I've been so excited about the opportunity. Especially after I went out there and spent time with everyone. And now it's like everything has been turned upside down. I don't know what to think."

Adela laid her delicate hand on Dottie's arm and patted. "You will. God hasn't brought you this far to leave you stranded. Do you believe that?"

Dottie nodded. "I did. No. I do. I really do believe that."

"Then why don't you use my phone and call your brother. Talk to him in person instead of on that computer and see if there are any other developments."

Dottie glanced at the phone sitting on the end of the counter and instantly longed for contact with her brother. It wasn't just the devastating news about the home being closed but also thoughts of Brady, too, that drove her to stand. "Thank you, Adela. I think that's exactly what I need."

"And this is exactly what I need. For an old woman, I like it when God can still use me." She smiled and her eyes twinkled like stars.

Dottie walked over to the phone as Adela's words echoed in her ears. *I like it when God can still use me...* He was using Adela, even tucked out here in the middle of nowhere. That was pretty impressive.

Lifting the phone from its dock, Dottie felt better.

Things would work out. God had a plan.

Even if it did seem like a maze right now and she was just a little mouse hunting for the right path.

Dottie was awakened the next morning by a knock on her RV door by one Gordon P. Rudy. Prudy for short. She'd felt once more as if God was smiling down on her as she dressed, then watched him haul her RV to his shop. However, that had been before he'd started digging around under the hood. The infuriating man had been at it for thirty minutes. He was like a human band. Whistling, humming and clucking. Whistling, clucking and humming.

Just about the time she thought he was going to say

something he'd throw her a weird look over his shoulder, shake his head then dive back in with a bout of rapid tinkering. It was getting on her nerves. "I don't know about this engine," he said suddenly, out of the blue. "There's not much left of her, not much at all."

"Are you sure?"

He zapped her with an inquiring gaze over the top of his grease-speckled glasses.

Okay, maybe that was a silly question. "I meant to say— It's burned up, but you can fix it. Right?"

He perked up at her confidence in his abilities. "Sure, I'll tear into it. But it might take me a day..." He paused, scratched his scraggly chin. "Or two. Truthfully, there ain't no guarantees. I might have to get a whole new engine. That could take a few days, even a week."

A week! Todd needed her in L.A. He'd assured her not to worry. When they'd spoken, his confidence radiated through the phone wires. Even with the short ten-day turnover time, he believed God would provide them with a new house. In the meantime, they were packing up and preparing for the move. Wherever it might be.

It had been the strangest thing, talking to him. She could still hear the fire in his voice when he'd said, "Dottie, it's when we have no answers that trusting the Lord is so exciting. That's when we actually see God shine!"

How quickly she'd forgotten. After all God had carried her through, she felt like the Hebrews out in the wilderness when miracle after miracle had protected them and still they'd forsaken the Lord. She'd been quick to judge their unfaithfulness. And now, after the miracles He'd worked in her own life, she'd done the same.

The realization had shamed her, but the prospect of seeing God at work again thrilled her.

She just had to get to L.A. to see it happen. Prudy was looking at her, one smudgy eyebrow wrinkled in question. Waiting for her to make some kind of observation. "A week, you say," she said, fighting her frenzied nerves. "So what you're telling me is that I may need to find other transportation out of here."

"Like I said, it may take me a few days, but then it should be ready to roll. One way or the other." He laughed at his humor, showing a wide mouth of teeth.

"What does that mean? One way or the other?" She lost the battle. Her nerves kicked in. "My brother needs me to help pack and move. They only have a few days to get relocated, and packing up four families is a lot of work." *Calm down, Dottie. Think.* "I need to rent a car."

"Now, ma'am—" Prudy wiped his hands on the

dirty brown work rag "—if you give me a day. Or two."
She tapped her toe, thinking. Norma Sue had already
invited her and Cassie to spend the night at her place
for as long as they needed, so a place to stay wasn't
any problem. She just needed to hit the road. "I'll give
you a day," she said. "I'll be back tomorrow to see
what you've come up with. Then I'm getting a rental
car. I can always come back for the RV, but day after
tomorrow, mark my words, this little gal will be in
L.A. And that's a promise."

Brady flicked his wrist, let the lasso twirl above his
head, watching the calf, feeling the expert moves of
his horse as it anticipated each motion of the calf.
There was nothing like the thrill of riding a highly
trained cutting horse. It was an experience that took
your mind away from everything except the powerful
motion of the horse as it hunkered down low, dug its
hooves into the dirt and skillfully directed the calf in
the way it should go. Letting the lasso fly, he snapped
the tension as soon as it settled around the calf's neck.
Brady was off the horse in a blink. Flipping the calf, he
snagged its feet and expertly wrapped them together.
"You beat your record," Clint called from his perch on
the gate, holding up a stopwatch. "Man, that was some

concentration."

Brady stepped away from the calf to take his hat from J.P. "Good ride, cowboy," the younger man said. Brady gave him a nod and slapped the dust off his hat onto his leg as he led his horse over to Clint, where he took a seat on the fence beside him.

He'd taken the day off, at least in theory. Everyone knew where to reach him in case of emergency.

After leaving Dottie at her RV the day before, he hadn't been able to think straight.

Had it really been less than a full week since she'd driven into his life? It was true, but hard to believe since it had become nearly impossible to imagine his life without her.

But he would. Soon.

Prudy was back in town and it was only a matter of hours before Dottie would realize leaving Mule Hollow might only be a phone call away. When Prudy explained how critical her RV's situation was, she'd call for a rental.

She'd leave in a moment. There was really nothing more she could do for Cassie. The kid was pretty much grown, with a definite mind of her own, and didn't seem to be a criminal. Mule Hollow was about the safest place in the world for her to choose as her residence.

There was nothing to keep Dottie in Mule Hollow anymore. The soft ring of her laughter drifted through his memory. Her smile rode on its crest.

Yesterday had proved that the tension between them was the product of feelings that ran deep. A connection he had no right to want to strengthen.

Dottie had been through too much, he could never ask her to take a chance on life with him.

He couldn't picture Dottie in the role of grieving widow.

Even though, despite his attempts to stop it from happening, he'd started picturing her in the role of his wife.

"Earth to Brady, man, you've got it bad."

Brady regarded his longtime friend. "No. I don't."

Clint lifted an eyebrow in answer. "Oh, yeah. You do. Believe me, I know the signs. I've been there."

Brady shot a glare at him. "Look, Clint, I came out here today to relax. Not to get a lecture on—" He broke off. Not wanting to voice what he had no business voicing.

"Love. Come on, buddy. This is me you're talking to. I was there when you got your first crush on Stella Benford."

"And that makes you a expert on my love life."

"You mean, your lack of a love life. Do you think I haven't noticed? Not that I wasn't where you are at one time. But Lacy changed that, my friend." He chuckled. Brady watched the chute open and the horse and rider charge out after the calf. Clint started the watch and clicked it off again when the cowboy missed his throw.

"You can't tell me that you're going to ignore what's happening between you and Dottie. She seems like a great gal. Everybody can see there's something going on between you two."

"Drop it, Clint, she's leaving. She has a life and it's not in Mule Hollow."

"Listen to me for a minute. I thank God every day for allowing that ball of trouble, Lacy Brown, to crash into my life. You saw her. You know how she shook up my world. It wasn't pretty. But she's the best thing that ever happened to me. You need your life shaken up, man. And you need to move mountains to make it happen if you have to."

"God's going to have to do that if anything is going to come of the feelings I have for Dottie Hart. Yeah—" he met the smile in Clint's eyes "—rub it in. You're right, I can't deny that I've never felt the way Dottie makes me feel. But the way I see it, that's all the more reason for me to protect her. Isn't that what a man is supposed to do? Protect the ones he loves—cares about. For me that's stopping it before it happens."

Clint laughed. "And what if God has different plans?"

Brady hopped from the fence. "He won't."

Dottie stopped by Heavenly Inspirations after leaving Prudy's to tell Lacy and Sheri that she would be leaving the next day. She'd forgotten Norma Sue and Esther Mae had informed her at dinner at Lilly's that they were going in for a little TLC on Monday morning. Just seeing them all together brought a sudden wave of regret. It had been such a short time, but she'd come to love them. She'd miss them.

"Lacy!" Esther Mae was shouting from beneath the dryer as Dottie stepped into the salon. The squeal in Esther's voice was hair-raising.

"You need to put one of them mud baths in here," she continued shouting. "I saw on the Travel Channel that women love to climb into a vat of that nasty-looking stuff but it must be good—"

"Ha! Esther Mae," Norma yelled back from where she sat in Lacy's chair. Lacy waved at Dottie and smiled a welcome instead of interrupting what promised to be an enlightening exchange. "I can just see me in a vat of mud!" She patted her ample belly. "It wouldn't be pretty. You telling me you'd pay to get in a tub of dirt and water?"

Esther Mae frowned. "Well, surely. It'd be one more thing to draw women to Mule Hollow. We could have one of those day spas. Get real classy like. Mud's not hard to come by and I grow cucumbers in my garden every year. We could use them specially grown for ladies' dark circles."

Norma harrumphed and shook her head. "Esther, listen what you're saying. That ain't just any kind of mud. It ain't like they just got some dirt and turned on the water hose."

"Well, Norma, I know that! That mud had sea salt from the Mediterranean—no, I think it was from the Dead Sea—no, wait, maybe it was the Nile."

Lacy chuckled. "Esther Mae, I might have to special order some mud just for you." She removed the cutting cape from Norma Sue. "You're a free woman, Norma Sue. Your turn, Dottie. How's it going this morning? You should have seen Cassie last night. That girl had more fun helping deliver that calf. Of course, poor Jake, that kid has it bad. He just beamed the entire time, explaining every little thing that was happening."

Dottie didn't know what to answer first. "I'm glad

she enjoyed it. That's what I came to talk to you about. I'm leaving tomorrow and I need to figure out what's going to happen to Cassie when I go."

Adela was sitting quietly getting her nails done, and by the expressions around the room she obviously hadn't said anything to anyone about their conversation the day before.

"You're leaving!" Norma exclaimed, grabbing the broom and sweeping her hair up off the floor.

"No, no, no," Lacy said, taking her by the arm and tugging her into the styling chair.

"Oh, boy," Sheri warned. "You're in for it now."

"Did someone die?" Esther Mae shouted, lifting the hood of the dryer.

Norma Sue swung around and snapped the dryer off. "You're driving me crazy, Esther Mae! Dottie just said she was leaving."

"But she can't leave! She has to marry Bra—"

"Esther Mae—"

"It's okay, Norma," Lacy said, spinning Dottie toward the mirror. "Let's let Dottie talk."

Dottie had known they all had high hopes that something would develop between her and Brady. But it wouldn't. She'd be lying if she said she didn't have feelings for him, because she did. She'd realized yesterday after their painful conversation that she was

188

falling in love with Brady Cannon. Who wouldn't? He had to be the most perfect man in the entire world…except he'd made up his mind to live his life alone…

Stop it. At the moment she didn't have time to think about herself. She had to get to California. Her friends needed her.

Taking a deep breath, she retold everything. From the loss of the lease to the excitement her brother was feeling that the Lord was going to provide for No Place Like Home.

When she finished speaking not a whisper was heard inside Heavenly Inspirations as Lacy, Esther Mae, Norma Sue, Sheri and Adela all stared at her with their mouths open.

And then pandemonium broke out!

CHAPTER FIFTEEN

"They should come here!" Esther Mae exclaimed, her freshly dried red hair shaking she was so excited. "Yep, yep, yep!" Lacy laughed. "It's the perfect solution!"

"You were right, Lacy," Norma gasped. "God had it under control the whole time, and here I was thinking our intuition had gotten its antennas crossed."

Sheri folded her arms and shook her head. "If you build it they'll come."

Lacy nodded at Sheri. "That's right. God is so full of surprises."

Dottie needed to sit down—but she already was. "Hey," she called out. "I'm sorry, but that wouldn't work."

Necks almost broke as heads whipped around. "Well, sure it will," Esther Mae declared.

Dottie stood, suddenly feeling nervous. "It's not that

simple, these women. They… They've been through so much. As wonderful as Mule Hollow is, it is too far away from where—from what they're used to."

"That's the beauty of it," Norma Sue sighed.

Norma Sue sighing—Dottie did a double take on that. "Look, maybe sometime for a visit. But it is not feasible to think they could relocate this far away from their homes and whatever little bits of family they have left." Dottie looked at Adela for help. Maybe she would back her up but Adela just smiled gently and said nothing.

"Dottie, Dottie!" Lacy exclaimed. "Do not tell me you really think that things happen by coincidence? No way, not this scenario—" She slapped her hand on her jutted hip and her baby blue eyes danced. "Come on now, replay everything that's happened to bring *you* to be in Mule Hollow, our little one-horse town, for just this moment!"

Dottie felt light-headed. The film in her head rolled, even though she didn't need it to—Cassie on the road that day, the newspaper clippings, the fire, the mechanic being out of town… "No. I'm sorry, I have to think about this." Three strides and she made it to the door, she had to get outside.

Adela's hand on her arm stopped her just before she stepped outside. "Turn it over to God."

Their eyes met, Dottie nodded and then she swept out into the fresh air and bright sunshine.

She turned right, her steps clipped as she hurried along the plank boardwalk. At the intersection she turned right again. In Mule Hollow there weren't many options. At the end of the boardwalk, where the edge of town gave way to endless pastureland, she stopped and stared as the road made a straight shot to the horizon then disappeared.

What was she running from?

The question came out of nowhere. Wiping a hand down her face, Dottie leaned her forehead against the porch post and stared down at her shoes. *Dear Father. I'm so confused. Am I thinking of my friends, of Stacy, Rose, Nive and Lynn?* She called them all by name. Picturing their faces and those of each of their children. *Or am I thinking of myself? Please show me the way.* Dottie watched the sun on the faraway horizon and she had to be honest. Mule Hollow would be a wonderful place for her friends. Rose had a thirteen-year-old son. He'd been struggling, and like Brady had told her over and over again about Cassie, Mule Hollow was the perfect place for a mixed-up kid. She knew everything they'd said was true. But she couldn't do it.

This was about Brady Cannon.

It was one thing for a woman to be falling for a man who never intended to get married—if that woman was moving on, riding off into the sunset, moseying off over the horizon to find a new life. A life where she stood a chance of forgetting the man who very easily could break her heart.

But…

It was an entirely different ending to that movie if the poor girl had to live in the same town with the guy. See him every day and pretend that she didn't long for exactly the life he'd turned his back on.

Oh my goodness! After all her professions of following God's lead, she was contemplating not giving her friends the opportunity to choose Mule Hollow as their new residence because of selfish personal reasons. The truth sank in and she closed her eyes in shame.

How low could she go?

Evidently pretty amazingly low.

What was she? A woman with a purpose? Or a mouse? Kicking away from the post, Dottie hurried back toward Main Street and hung a left and nearly tripped when she saw Lacy and the others standing outside the salon watching for her.

"Okay," she snapped. "Give me a phone and let's make this call. Forgive me for being small-minded and selfish. I have to give them the option at least."

Everyone started talking at once. It was decided to head over to Sam's and have a huddle to hammer out details before making the call. As Adela pointed out, they needed to figure out where to put everyone if they decided to move to Mule Hollow.

Dottie sobered at that bit of detail, but actually felt better thinking about it. There was still a chance that Mule Hollow wasn't the place for No Place Like Home. The ball wasn't in her court at all. Housing for this endeavor would have to be provided and that put the ball completely in the Lord's hands.

Brady held the door of Sam's Diner. Despite his better judgment he'd come to town to invite Dottie to lunch. She would be leaving soon and he didn't see what spending time with her would hurt. There was a good chance that after tomorrow he'd never see her again. It was hard to think about. But he knew it was for the best.

But Clint hadn't helped temper the yearning his heart was feeling.

Brady had left his friend's ranch longing for Dottie's company. What could lunch hurt? He found the RV at Prudy's after remembering he was back to fix it. The mechanic spared no detail about how Dottie was leaving town. Whatever. The girl still had to eat lunch. He'd try Sam's. He just hadn't expected to see Sam's packed.

His heart seemed to swell when right there in the middle of the group, he spotted Dottie.

"Brady Cannon!" Lacy exclaimed. "You're just in time. We need all the brain cells we can gather on this big news."

"And what's that?" He removed his hat and hooked it on the peg by the door. Needing the distraction to refocus on something other than the way Dottie's eyes had sparked when their gazes met, or the memories of their mudding expedition, he took a seat at the counter. With his back to her.

"We need a house," Norma Sue called out. "A big house. What do you think about the Nelson house? You remember, it's out on Fullson Road. They had those four adorable kids. Their place was pretty nice, 'course it's been setting vacant for years, like all the houses out here."

"Norma, that house might work," Adela said. "It's been years since I've been out there, though. Have any of you seen it lately?"

Brady had. "I was out that way a week ago."

"Yeah, what kind of shape is it in?" Esther Mae

asked.

Esther Mae was not one to be able to curb her enthusiasm and Brady could hear the excitement in her voice. What were these gals up to now? If there was one thing the men of Mule Hollow had learned, it was that when there was a gathering at Sam's of the women of Mule Hollow, something was up. However, the house they were talking about was off the market as of last week. But he didn't have the right to tell anyone the particulars. He turned to face the room of ladies.

"It's in fair shape," he said, curious. "What's up?"

"We're looking for a house for Dottie's friends in California. Their lease didn't get renewed and now they have less than nine days to get out. No Place Like Home is coming to Mule Hollow—"

"Now, Esther Mae," Dottie broke in, her voice breathless, cautious. "We don't know that for certain. We still have to invite them. And find a house."

Brady had stalled on the information. "You mean Dottie isn't leaving?" Now, why'd he go and blurt that out? Every knowing set of eyeballs in the room turned on him. Sam's included.

"Not if we can help it," Lacy sang. She had a tendency to do that when she thought romance was on the wind. He'd learned to be wary of her singing. "We're making the case to her that Mule Hollow is the

196

best place in the world for a group of women wanting to start a new life. You know, good old cowboy hospitality!"

He met Dottie's gaze, she wasn't smiling.

"So what brought this on?" he asked, choking on the coffee Sam had filled his cup with, coffee that only accelerated the drumming of his heart. Dottie staying. He'd faced death many times in his career as a city cop, pulling people out of burning cars, mangled wrecks with leaking gas tanks... Once he'd run into a burning building and carried an old man to safety, but the thought of facing Dottie every day and trying to hide his love for her...well, that was the scariest thing he'd ever faced.

And he'd realized that he did love her. Right this very minute.

"That house is not on the market," he managed to say.

"What?" Norma Sue barked. "Since when?"

"Last week."

"Last week!" Esther Mae beat everyone else to the exclamation. "Who bought it?"

He cleared his throat. "I'm not at liberty to say."

"To say what?" Molly Popp asked, entering the diner.

Brady was certainly not at liberty to say anything

to Molly. The cowboy who'd bought the place had specifically said he didn't want to see anything about his buying a ranch in her weekly newspaper article. The guy had a point. Molly didn't mean any harm with her column; it had been great for the most part. But everything that happened in Mule Hollow didn't have to be reported to her faithful readers. With that in mind, Brady honored his friend's wishes and said nothing.

"We need a big house," Esther Mae told Molly. "But Brady just informed us the one we thought might work has sold. Sold right beneath our noses and we didn't have a clue. Who is it?"

Brady shook his head. "Now, Esther, you know I can't break a confidence. Much as I'd like to fill you in on the surprise, it's not my call."

Esther Mae scowled. "That just ain't right."

"Okay," Lacy said. "Then let's move on. Adela, Norma and Esther—oh, and Sam, you're in on this, too. You and Brady, you have lived here longer that me or Sheri, so think where there is a house that's big enough to house four women and their children? We don't want to split them up. Mule Hollow is about to get the privilege to minister to these women's needs, spiritually, emotionally…this is a huge and seriously awesome undertaking."

Brady was listening to Lacy, but out of the corner of his eye, he could see Sheri quietly explaining the whole story to Molly. You could tell Molly'd already started writing her next article.

"What about Brady's house?"

He almost didn't hear Adela's soft suggestion. Then it hit him. My house! *"My house!"* he exclaimed, suddenly struck by the fact that the last fifteen minutes had been full of exclamations. But once the shock of the suggestion settled, he let it sink in. It would be perfect. "Miss Adela," Dottie gasped. "That's Brady's house. He lives there."

Brady met her faltering gaze. "Actually, it's a good suggestion."

CHAPTER SIXTEEN

"**B**rady, can I see you outside?" Dottie snapped, shooting out of her chair. The man was not giving up his house! How crazy was that?

Without complaint he followed her onto the front step of Sam's. "What do you think you're doing?"

He dipped his chin. "I'm trying to help. I only said that Adela was right. My house is big enough. The good Lord knows I don't use it. It's a good idea."

"No. It's not."

"Why? They need a place to go. Didn't someone say they had very few days to get out? Did you know this was coming?"

"Yes, they have only nine days left, and no, I didn't know. Well, not technically. I knew the lease was coming up at the end of the month and I knew there was a chance that the owner might not renew. But…"

Dottie leaned against the wall with a sigh. "Honestly, Brady, I never expected that God would allow that door to close. That He would put them out in the street like this. I think I was in denial. I mean, why would He let this happen? They were doing so well."

Brady's hand on her cheek surprised her.

"Dottie, take a breath and relax. I'll be the first to tell you that I don't understand or always like what God does. But the bottom line is that He can do what He wants. I'm thinking that maybe this could be a good move for them, based on what you've told me."

"That's basically what Miss Adela told me." She was trying to ignore the effect his touch was having on her. He pushed her hair behind her ear, then let his hand rest on the wall behind her head. His closeness was distracting, her stomach was flipping again. "I'm not denying that it could be a good move. But I haven't even suggested it to them yet."

"Why?" He lifted an eyebrow, his eyes searching hers.

"I…" She couldn't very well tell him that *he* was her problem. "Well, I think that if this is God's plan, He'll provide the house. So you don't have to sacrifice your home. Todd is so excited to see what God is going to provide. He doesn't act like he's worried in the least. So I'm thinking positive like he is. I mean, it's not like

I haven't seen God work in miraculous ways. I'm a walking testament to His power. Still, I don't want to suggest Mule Hollow unless He gives me the perfect place. That way I'll know for certain He's in on the plan. I wouldn't want to offer a solution that wasn't right. Do you see?" She'd been talking ninety miles an hour. Brady started nodding his head halfway through her spiel.

He studied her face, his expression intense. "God *has* provided. My house is the right one. You know it is. I have my parents' original home down by the river. I've been thinking about it recently—it's perfect for me. I'm never going to need that rambling house. With me out of the way, it has the chance to actually become what it was intended for when it was built. Do you get what I'm saying?"

Dottie pushed away from him and walked to stare across the street, through tear-filled eyes. She got exactly what he was saying. He would continue his solitary march.

He came to stand behind her. She could feel his breath on her hair.

"I won't ever change my mind."

She breathed in a calming breath and willed her heart to settle down as she closed her eyes and let everything sink in.

Doors closed and windows opened.

If everyone was right, God was in on this. He'd taken the ball and handed her His solution. As much as she wanted to deny it, Brady was right. There was no place like his home and it would be the perfect location for her friends. Still, she had to give it one more shot. "It's not right."

"Yes, it is. And you know it."

Despite everything, she spun toward him and planted her hand squarely on his chest. "You need children. A wife. You need to—" He took her hand from his chest.

"I've made my mind up. I'm moving out of the main house. With or without the shelter moving into it. Dottie, I hate going home to that giant. I've needed to do this for a long time."

Looking at his hand holding hers, she hurt for what he was giving up. But she felt as if she was being swept downstream by too strong a current.

"Then I guess all that's left to do is to make a call."

Within the hour it had been decided. They were coming. Dottie hadn't expected the wholehearted enthusiasm the suggestion elicited from all four women. They all jumped at the chance to give their children a fresh start in what sounded to them like the perfect town. There was hope in their response.

And with that response Dottie realized she was doing the right thing. Her coming to Mule Hollow had not been an accident. And yet no matter how she tried she couldn't summon up the joy she knew she should be feeling, knowing that her friends would now have a place to call theirs again.

It was decided Todd would have his church load the moving van, then he would drive them out. There were formalities that needed to be handled, and paperwork that needed to be signed, but Todd didn't anticipate any problems. He wouldn't be making the move himself, as he felt his place was still in L.A. Therefore, Pastor Allen of Mule Hollow's Church of Faith stepped up as spiritual adviser. The town of Mule Hollow would also establish an advisory board and take on some of the funding for the ministry.

And, just like that, it had been settled.

They would be arriving in six days. It wasn't much time to prepare for them, but it would have to do.

Brady's house was attacked that very afternoon by the Mule Hollow Clean Team! Every available female converged on Brady's home to give it a going-over and to decide what needed to be done to make it work for its soon-to-be residents.

Poor Brady, he'd made the offer and then Dottie was forced to watch him basically be kicked out of his home. He acted as if it didn't matter to him. But it had to. Dottie refused to believe he was walking away without some smidgen of regret.

Yet as the day ended and he moved out for good, it was quite obvious that no one else thought the same thing.

Brady tossed his duffel bag on the floor next to the front door and surveyed his new home. It had been six months since he'd been inside. Dust everywhere hung like a dark cloud over everything, not unlike the one hanging over his head. Dottie and the other ladies had wanted to come clean for him, but he'd told them no. They needed to focus on getting everything else ready for the shelter.

He was okay with moving into the cabin. With its wooden floors and plank walls and the rustic furnishings, it was the ultimate guy habitat. He'd spent the first six years of his life here before the big house had been built. In his later years it had been a favorite retreat for him and his buddies. No, glancing around the familiar room, his dark mood had nothing to do with the surroundings and everything to do with wondering how to handle the issue of his heart.

Grabbing a rag from the drawer in the kitchen and a bottle of spray wax, he attacked the coffee table. Frankly, he was glad to have the busywork, trying to rid his mind of everything as he rubbed this way and that way. Wax on. Wax off…

…and what if God has different plans? Clint's words played through his mind, overriding his wax job. Had it really only been that morning that Clint had asked him that question?

He won't. What a pompous answer he'd thrown out there. God could do whatever He wanted to do. Which led him to the real reason for his bad mood—*Lord, what's going on?*

He'd admitted that he loved Dottie.

He'd admitted it straight out to himself and to Clint. He'd also said God was going to have to change things in order for him to see his responsibilities differently.

Well, He'd changed things all right!

Never in his wildest dreams had he entertained the idea that things could change this drastically this fast. It was as if God had heard him snap his smart-aleck "He won't" retort to Clint, took it as a challenge and said, "Let me show you exactly who I am and what I can do."

What he'd thought was a pretty cut-and-dried life path had now turned into the ultimate quandary.

"Who knew how much dust could accumulate in four years?" Esther Mae coughed.

Dottie glanced her way and fought not to laugh. Esther was crouched on all fours peering under the bed. Well, she wasn't exactly peering; she'd crammed herself beneath the bed frame as far as she could get, leaving her lower half sticking up in the air, as she struggled to reach something. As Dottie watched, she plopped flat down on the carpet on her belly and scooted as far as she could go under the bed, attempting to reach her target.

"Gotcha!" she exclaimed at last. Then, maneuvering out, she sat up holding a dusty shoe. How long it had been under the bed was anyone's guess.

Dottie couldn't help smiling. Brady was a bachelor. He lived mostly in his room on the first floor. It was obvious from all the dust that he seldom ventured upstairs.

To see these rooms utilized would be good. To see life in the home that his parents had built for just that reason would be a fulfillment to a dream...of sorts. That was what kept her going. Kept her from feeling sick over Brady's seemingly concrete decision to never have a family.

The task of cleaning and clearing was a good-size job, but everyone had shown up to help.

And everyone had one goal: to help their new friends from California.

"This could be it," Esther Mae said, slapping at the cobweb hanging from her flaming-red hair. "These poor battered souls could be just what Mule Hollow has been waiting for. Just think about it, they need husbands and we have cowboys. And I would dearly love to hear the laughter of kids on our streets again."

"That would be nice," Norma Sue added, coming into the room. "Years ago, when the oil-field workers lived here and we were a thriving little town, it was wonderful. Kids playing in front of their homes or riding bicycles along the streets was natural."

Esther sighed. "I miss that. When the oil drilling stopped and all our friends and families who'd been supported by that work moved away, it was terrible." She blinked and met Dottie's gaze. "We knew we were in trouble. And look where we ended up, a dried-up old dust bowl out in the middle of nowhere. But things are perking up every time someone new moves to town. This is so exciting! To think that in one moment this house could be…well, it could be like a holding tank. You know, before we marry them off!" She snapped the shoe, sending up a plume of dust.

"Esther. Woman! Get a hold of yourself," Norma Sue yelped. "They don't need you marrying them off first thing. They haven't even arrived and you're marrying them off already. What they need most right now is a home to call their own, a place to feel safe. And who knows, they may take one look at this one-horse town and run back to the city."

Lacy reached out and hugged Esther Mae, sneezing as she did. "I'm excited, too, Esther, but this is all part of God's plan, so just let it happen naturally. Also, ladies, lunch is about ready, so we need to move 'um out. Adela and Sam have the spread all laid out downstairs. They have fixed enough to feed an army. One thing's for certain, we won't fizzle out on this job from lack of fuel."

They were following Lacy out the bedroom door when suddenly she spun around, slammed her hands to the doorframe and glared at them, all wild-eyed and grinning. "By George, I think I've got it!" she exclaimed. "Dottie, I can see it. We've been trying to figure out for months now a business that Mule Hollow could invest in. A business that could employ women.

Remember the first day we met you and I mentioned us needing a restaurant? Duh! We've been praying about it all this time…and it's been here under our noses for days and I'm just now getting it! You are the answer to our prayers!"

"Hey, Lacy, you're right," Esther Mae agreed.

Norma Sue grinned. "Not just one business but two—"

"Right, Norma," Lacy said. "Dottie, your candy is wonderful. Everyone was talking about it at the Trade Days. We could start a line of candies, distribute them all over the place. A restaurant wouldn't work because we have Sam's, but maybe a bakery. It could work. Molly's articles have paved the way. Do you know how many people are reading those articles she's writing? Oh, my goodness, I see it. If we put it out there, they're going to buy it."

Sheri entered the room from where she'd been cleaning across the hall. Her trademark smirk was on her face, a sure sign she'd heard everything. "All I have to say to you, Dottie Hart, is you'd better get ready to run."

Dottie swallowed. "Why?" It came out as a squeak. She gave Dottie a "duh" look, similar to the one

Cassie had given her on their first meeting. "Girlfriend! Don't tell me you haven't realized that you just lost control of your life."

"No, she hasn't," Norma Sue objected with a huff. "All we're saying is this is the perfect solution to our problem. If we start a candy business we could employ women. With its success we can offer employment, enabling more women to settle here. There's something to be said for being able to pay your bills."

Lacy plopped her hand on her jutting hip, her eyes bright as headlights. "Dottie, with you at the helm, directing our endeavor, we could go all the way. Food is the way to any man's heart. We get a bunch of women cooking, and *bingo!*" She snapped her fingers. "Those cowboys will be dropping like flies."

Sheri lowered her chin and raised her eyebrows as she mouthed, "Told ya."

Dottie gave a weak smile. What else could she do?

"You girls move fast. I feel like I'm on a roller coaster and can't get off."

"Tell me about it," Sheri said. "I'm telling you, these ol' gals can put the moves on you before you can blink an eyeball. Weren't we supposed to be eating?"

"Yep, yep," Lacy laughed. "Come on, we'll talk more downstairs."

Dottie realized as everyone filed downstairs that she hadn't been in control of her life for the last twenty-four hours—no, the last week. At least that was the way it felt. When everyone else went toward the food, she went the opposite direction. She needed space rather than food.

Space to think. And to pray.

CHAPTER SEVENTEEN

The barn was quiet when Dottie entered. She'd had to purposefully skirt the pile of cars in the driveway in order not to run into anyone in her quest for some solitude. It helped that everyone had stampeded toward the back porch to eat. Spying a hay bale in the corner, she was about to take a seat, when she saw Cassie.

She was sitting on a mean-looking piece of machinery that Dottie felt pretty sure attached to a tractor in some fashion. What the dangerous-looking thing did on the tractor she didn't have a clue—but it made a great bench, sitting at the back opening of the barn, facing the pasture and the trees.

Dottie took a deep breath, time alone could wait. "Mind if I sit for a while?"

Cassie swung her head around, startled that she'd

been found. But she shook her head and gazed back out across the pasture without saying anything.

A breeze was blowing. Dottie could smell the scent of dry hay as it drifted around the corner of the barn.

"Cassie, would you like to talk? I hope you know you can trust me."

At first she made no move to show whether she'd even heard Dottie or not. Then at last she took a shuddery breath.

"I am nineteen, Dottie. I really am. I can show you my ID if you want."

Dottie felt like a toad again. "That's okay. I believe you. I really do." And she did. "Do you want to talk about this thing with Bob and Jake? Something else is going on, isn't it?"

Cassie gave her a sideways glare. "Why? What's it to you if there is?"

Dottie had never wanted to give anyone a hug as much as she wanted to hug Cassie. She wasn't certain she'd ever known anyone who might actually need a hug more than Cassie. Or, who might reject it as quickly. So she opted simply to smile and speak from her heart. "Cassie, I hope more than anything that you know I'm your friend."

She met Dottie's gaze, bright and raw with fiercely restrained emotion. "Yeah. I know." She blinked and looked away, relaxing faintly. "Hey, these women that are coming, their kids are gonna need a few things. I was wondering, could I borrow a few bucks? I'm going to ride to Ranger with Bob. He's going to take me by the store, but I don't have any money. I'll work and pay you back. Sam said I could start working for him a few hours a day, so I'm gonna start tomorrow. That means I can pay you back at the end of the week."

Dottie adjusted to the about-face. She'd hoped Cassie would open up, but ever since she'd realized that something from Cassie's past was forcing her actions, Dottie couldn't bring herself to rush the girl. "Sure, I'll give you the money. But you don't need to pay me back. You helped me with the candy for the Trade Days."

"No, that was to pay you back for bringing me here. I'll pay you for the stuff at the end of the week."

Dottie's admiration for the girl grew. "I brought you here because I wanted to. Let me go get my purse." She got up to go. "You're sure you don't want to talk?" She had to try.

"Dottie, Bob will make the perfect husband. You'll see."

"Does Bob know you're thinking of him like this?"

She shook her head. "No. I have to give him time

to fall in love with me. And he will. I know it. He's just my friend right now. We discussed that the other day. He told me he liked me, that I was a good kid… of course, he has to get to know me and realize I can be more than that. I'm not a kid."

"And Jake, I thought when you went mudding with him the other day, maybe you were switching—"

"I don't want to talk about Jake. I'm actually crazy about Jake. He's fun—" She looked away, blinking hard. "But it takes more than fun to make a husband."

"Can't you just relax on the husband thing? You have your entire life ahead of you. God has a man out there for you, so you don't have to rush. His timing is perfect."

"Don't." She shot to her feet, her expression livid.

Her eyes glittered with rage.

Dottie gasped. Why had she pushed? She'd known better. She'd known better.

"All my life, the only thing I wanted was a family of my own. And a place, a perfect place to live with that family and it's here. That's not too much to ask. If God loves me so much, like you and Miss Adela keep trying to tell me, then He'll give me what I want one day. His timing… So far, His timing stinks."

Spinning away, she stormed toward the entrance of the barn, her thin shoulders shaking. Her pain sliced

Dottie to the core. *Dear Lord, what had happened to Cassie?* Some deep pain drove everything that girl did, Dottie knew clearly now.

She had to talk to Brady.

Scrambling off her perch, she hurried from the barn, passing Jake on the way. He was standing near the house talking to Clint about building a sandbox for the toddlers. Though he was talking to Clint, she could see his gaze lingering on Cassie, who was now standing at the corner of the barn watching a cow in the pen swat flies with its tail. She made a heart-wrenching picture. Dottie found her purse, pulled out fifty dollars, but before she headed back out to give it to Cassie, she sought out Bob. He was standing near his truck, taking orders on the different things he needed to pick up at the lumberyard to build the playground. Dottie was glad because Brady's house needed a playground. It looked as if it were wishing for one ever since it had been built.

The fact that it should be Brady's children playing on the playground flitted through her mind, but instead she focused on the situation at hand.

Why was Bob asking Cassie to ride to town with him?

She'd thought they had an understanding, but it didn't include this closeness that appeared to be happening between the two of them. He needed to be warned that the situation was even more delicate than she'd realized.

However, before she had time to say anything, Cassie jogged up.

"Hey, Dottie, you got the cash?" All trace of her anger and tears was gone. One would never know she'd just been upset.

Dottie handed her the money and she took it, met her gaze and smiled.

"Thanks," she said, stuffing the bills into her jeans while hurrying around to climb into the passenger seat of the truck. "Okay, Bob baby, let's hit the road."

Bob glanced at Brady then at Dottie and lifted an eyebrow. "Cassie said you needed her to pick up a few things."

Dottie heard the question in his voice. "Well, I—"

"Hop to, Bob, time's a-wastin'." Cassie bounced in the seat and thumped the side of the door where she had an arm hung out the window.

Bob sighed. "We'll be back. On the quick side."

"So, what was that all about?" Brady asked, coming up beside her and watching them pull out of the driveway.

"I'm not sure, she just asked if she could borrow some money. It seemed really important to her to buy something for the kids. The question is, what's up with Bob offering to take her—"

Brady dipped his chin and looked at her from beneath the shadow of his Stetson. It was a "just how slow are you?" kind of look.

Oh man! She should have known. "He didn't offer, did he? She told him I needed her to pick up something so she could go along with him to town!"

Brady laughed, nodding. "I think we've all been hoodwinked."

CHAPTER EIGHTEEN

Brady watched the emotions play across Dottie's face as she watched Bob and Cassie pull out onto the paved road, headed toward Ranger. He had to concede that Cassie was tenacious and creative, but his heart felt heavy looking at Dottie. She wore her heart on her sleeve, and her concern for the girl was touching. But the kid would be okay, and Bob and Jake would live.

He wasn't so sure about himself.

How was he going to live in the same town with Dottie? See her walking down the street, sitting in the pew, standing on his porch, hear her laughter…

You just will.

That didn't mean it would be easy. Every second around her made it harder.

Watching her work so hard to make this ministry

happen brought an even greater level of respect to the feelings he had for Dottie. She worked endlessly, she was tired and even now she was hurting. He'd noticed her slight limp as she'd come up the path earlier. Most people wouldn't notice, because it was so faint. But he noticed everything about her. And he knew her hip had to be hurting pretty bad or she'd be able to hide the limp. The way she usually did.

That he could see even the slightest indication of one meant she was fighting hard to hide the pain or just too tired to fight it.

The woman never complained. Despite her injuries and the discomfort they still caused her, she gave her all to everything in her life.

That had been proven with the way she felt for Cassie. Her heart was expansive…he wondered if she'd always been this way or if this was a product of what she'd lived through. He couldn't imagine her any other way.

"Did you eat?" he asked. She turned toward him, glancing one last time toward the road where the truck had disappeared, then shook her head.

"Haven't made it over there yet. Listen, Cassie is telling the truth about being nineteen. I believe her completely. But her head is really mixed up when it comes to this thing she has about chasing Bob. There is something in her background fueling her every move. To her, Bob represents more stability, with his age and all."

"You're probably right. Maybe her home life was less than desirable. It happens every day."

Dottie looked thoughtful. "That's what I'm thinking."

"Well, there's nothing you can do about it right now. And you've been working like a team of ten men. So we're going to get you some food, then find a place for you to rest that hip." Her expression of surprise was comical. "Don't look so surprised. I have eyes. Now, come on, you have to see the spread that Adela and Sam fixed."

There wasn't anything he could do for Cassie at that moment, but he could take care of Dottie.

Still looking perplexed and worried, she fell into step beside him. "Adela and Sam have fixed a feast," he said again.

After a moment of silence she cleared her throat. "I'm curious…are they…what would be the word? Are they courting? They never say anything, yet I can tell they're close."

Brady nodded, more than glad that she'd changed the subject. "It's something that's been building for years, but as far as anyone can tell it'll continue to build and never materialize."

"That's sad."

He paused at the corner of the house. They could see Adela and Sam standing behind the table they'd set up on the back patio. Sam loved Adela. Everyone could see it. But he'd never stepped over the line that he'd drawn for himself. It was sad, but what a man did with his life was his business. "Sam must have his reasons." Dottie studied the two dishing up food. They worked well together and it was obvious the wiry man adored Adela. They were opposites of each other, Adela with her elegant genteel grace and Sam with his brisk "take me or leave me" attitude. Brady wondered what Sam's story was.

What held him back from having what he wanted? Dottie walked ahead of him toward the table, and he couldn't help wondering if his fears had merit after all. Every moment he was near her put another chink in his armor.

The moving truck and the van pulled onto Main Street about four o'clock on Friday afternoon. But the small crowd gathered outside Sam's went bonkers.

Esther Mae was so excited she could barely speak. Dottie thought that might be one for the *Guinness Book of World Records* it was so odd.

Then there was Norma Sue, who looked like a mother hen about to be reunited with her baby chicks. She'd about worn a hole in the plank walk outside Sam's. She'd been marching back and forth in front of the diner with one eye glued to the street, waiting for the van to appear. When it finally came around the corner, she hollered and actually jumped off the ground—not too high, but still, she did get a little air time and that counted for a woman built with the same aerodynamics as a bumblebee.

When the van came to a halt there was a mad rush toward it. Dottie was laughing when Todd hopped out and engulfed her in a bear hug.

"It's good to see you, little sister. Just seeing the town on the horizon made us all bust into smiles."

Dottie hugged him hard, so glad to see him. "I did the same thing when I saw it. But just wait until you meet everyone. They're the people who make Mule Hollow special." Todd released her and started shaking hands with the many being thrust his way.

"Stacy!" Dottie wrapped her arms around the thin blonde who ventured from the van first. The expression of awe on her face blessed Dottie. She prayed Stacy found peace in Mule Hollow. It was a prayer Dottie was praying for several, including herself.

"Come on, give us all a hug," Norma Sue blurted out, her arms open wide. Stacy hesitated, then let Norma engulf her as Dottie turned back to the others, hugging each woman who stepped from the van. Chaotic introductions were made, hugs exchanged, and chatter ensued.

"Hey, baby," Esther cooed to the little boy peeking from around the van's seat. His blue gaze blinked, lifted to the top of her head and rolled to her feet then back up. When he timidly lifted his arms out to Esther, the poor woman teared up, enveloped the curly-headed boy in an embrace and lifted him from the van. "Ohhhh, I could just eat you up, you little doll."

"That's Gavin," Lynn said, smiling broadly. "And this is Jack."

Jack's hair was dark and straight, his eyes midnight blue. He followed his brother's lead and held his arms out. Norma Sue swept him up and dashed into Sam's before anyone else could steal him away from her. Adela, who'd been patiently waiting, stepped up and took baby Bryce from Stacy as she eased him from his car seat. She spoke her welcome, patting Stacy's hand, then followed the others into the cool interior of the restaurant. Stacy was left standing alone beside the van. Dottie watched as she soaked everything in. Dottie had expected to see more wariness from the young woman. But what she saw was curiosity and…wonder. Carefully avoiding eye contact with the few cowboys whose schedules had allowed them to be there,

Stacy scanned the streets with slow appreciation. Then she turned toward Sam's.

"Can…can I go in and look?" she asked.

In her letters, Stacy had asked many questions about the diner. "Sure you can." Dottie waved toward the door. "They have a feast ready for all of you in there. Believe me, they want you to go in. Be sure to stick a nickel in the jukebox and see what it feels like playing today."

She smiled then, it was a soft timid turn of the lips, hesitant, but struggling and brave. Dottie fought back tears. This girl had been through so much and here she was with eyes full of hope.

"Go on, I'll be there in just a moment."

Stacy nodded, her gaze floating back to Sam's. "Okay. I'll see you in a minute."

She'd started up the steps when a diaper slipped from the small bag slung over her shoulder. A group of cowboys had been standing respectfully to the side, hats in hands. Now, one of them broke from the pack like a knight in shining armor and scooped up the diaper.

"Miss, you dropped this," he said kindly.

Stacy turned and looked from him to the diaper he held up to her, where she was standing on the plank sidewalk. The man wasn't one of Mule Hollow's dashingly handsome cowboys. Instead, he was a lanky, too-thin, red-faced, bashful sort with a hesitant smile and kind, shy eyes. Dottie didn't know who looked most afraid. Stacy or the cowboy.

"Thank you," Stacy said, barely above a whisper, reaching uneasily for the diaper, looking away at the same time.

"Welcome to Mule Hollow, Miss. I— We're glad you're here. I—" he swallowed hard "—I'm glad you're here."

Stacy's skittish gaze moved to the group of men and back to him and she nodded hesitantly. "Thank you." Then accepting the diaper, she disappeared into the diner. The shy cowboy lingered, staring at the swinging door for a full minute before he walked away.

Wishing with all her heart that the scene could have been one of carefree ease and flickers of interest, Dottie turned back toward the others, who were laughing at something Lacy was telling them, waving her hands in the air and talking faster than the speed of light.

It looked like things might work out fine.

A shaggy-headed youth was the last off the van, climbing from the back row looking as if he'd been sleeping. Rose introduced him as her son, Max. He took one hard look at everyone, spun on his heel and stalked away.

Dottie's heart went out to the kid, but she didn't know what to do for him. Brady was watching the boy, too. She caught his gaze and for a moment, understanding pulsed between them, and yet there was a steady unease growing between them. Dottie looked back toward Max, uncertain what to do for the thirteen-year-old.

It was Cassie who broke from the flock to follow Max. She jogged after him and said something that made him stop. After a few words they continued walking at a slower pace. Talking. The girl had been distant since she'd come back from Ranger with Bob. She'd not tried to talk again and Dottie didn't really know if she should push the kid or cut her some slack. In the end she'd cut her the slack. Call her a coward, but Dottie just didn't know the right approach to something like this.

"Dottie," Rose said, stepping up beside her. "Max isn't too happy about the move. I'd guess because of the trouble he was having in school, he'd be happy to start fresh."

"He'll be fine. Cassie knows how he feels, in a way." The unmistakable sound of Jake's big truck cranking up drew her attention. As he passed them, he smiled a small smile down at her from his high seat, tipped his hat then continued at a slow crawl. Dottie's heart gave a kick.

When he pulled up beside Cassie and Max, he spoke to them and slowed to a stop. Even from where she and Rose stood it was evident that whatever he'd said brought a huge smile to Max's face. The tires on the truck were almost as tall as Max and it was evident he was impressed with what he saw.

"I wonder what he said," Rose gasped. "Max hasn't smiled like that in so long."

Dawning hit Dottie when Cassie and Max climbed up into the huge truck.

"I believe it probably had something to do with mud."

Rose clasped her hands together and her knuckles turned white. Suddenly feeling tremendously optimistic, Dottie hugged Rose. "Max is in good hands. Believe me, Mule Hollow may just be the place to make him start smiling all the time."

The hope reflected in Rose's eyes was beautiful. In

that moment Dottie wanted to take the goodhearted young cowboy and hug him until she couldn't hug anymore. Jake was twenty and could have ignored Max. But, like Cassie, he'd seen a hurting kid and he'd zeroed in on making the boy's arrival special. He knew the way to a boy's heart.

All Dottie could think watching that truck disappear down the road was, if Cassie couldn't see Jake was a jewel worth grabbing, then the girl wasn't anywhere near as smart as Dottie believed her to be.

CHAPTER NINETEEN

Dottie couldn't sleep. The twin bed in the room she shared with Cassie was comfortable enough, but tonight her mind was reeling with thoughts she'd been holding off by keeping busy. Very busy.

It had been two weeks since they'd all moved into Brady's home. The house now contained the women's shelter, but to Dottie it still belonged to Brady. Everywhere she looked she saw him. It was hard to think about him without wishing...but that wasn't what she needed to be doing, so she concentrated on making sure everyone else felt safe and happy. They needed her.

Tonight, though, things she'd been blocking were fighting for exposure.

In the incandescent glow of the moon, her gaze settled on the playground the men had built for the children of the house. It was useless—it was still Brady's children she envisioned playing there…her children.

Stop it, Dottie! Stop it.

This was ridiculous.

Everything was going great. At first she'd been nervous when Todd returned to L.A., but God's plans were working out unbelievably well! She'd started her cooking classes immediately, and she was having so much fun teaching. Brady's kitchen was as perfect for it as she'd known it would be. They were producing and learning and having fun doing it. The house was filled with laughter and hope. Even Stacy spoke more and more these days…not much, but more. Dottie took every good thing she could—one extra syllable out of Stacy's mouth was a step in the right direction.

And the cowboys, well, what could she say? The whole lot of them were supporting the candy business like starving men. You'd have thought they'd never been exposed to sweets before now. She was distributing the candy through Sam's Diner at the moment and having difficulty keeping him stocked. As a matter of fact, if business continued at this pace there would be a revolt. A horse revolt. They were going to bolt for the hills when their riders started waddling toward them.

It was time to open a storefront. Fat cowboys meant money.

No Place Like Home had a shot at supporting itself at this rate. So why couldn't she be happy?

A firefly glistened across the night sky on a lazy looping flight into the woods. A reminder of the man who lived through the trees in a cabin by the river all alone.

Brady. How she missed him.

Their contact with each other had been limited.

She'd known he worked a lot. It wasn't until she'd moved into his home that she realized exactly how little time the man actually spent off duty.

Either his job kept him busier than she'd realized or he was avoiding her. She'd been wondering about that. Despite efforts not to think about Brady, the man lurked consistently at the edge of her every thought.

She hadn't seen him much and yet the tension between them hadn't dissipated. If anything, it had grown. She found herself longing for his smile, longing to see the way his brown silken eyes seemed to see light when they were talking. Longing to hear his laughter. Longing to look up at him and believe that if she was going to be living in Mule Hollow indefinitely, that there was a chance that he could change his mind. That they had a chance at sharing a life together—the screen door creaked, startling Dottie from thoughts better left alone.

"Dottie. Can we talk?" Cassie whispered.

She, too, had been busy lately. She had been spending lots of time with Max and Jake. They'd taken the kid under their wing. Jake had been taking them to work with him on Clint's ranch after Max got home from school in the afternoons. During the day, when Cassie wasn't helping out down at the diner, she'd been helping with the candy making and the toddlers who were being babysat at the church. They'd both been so busy that there hadn't been too much one-on-one talk between them. Dottie had actually been relieved about that. For some reason, the girl had relented slightly on chasing poor Bob. Actually, she hadn't had much choice, because Bob had been scarce lately. He'd obviously decided to hang low for a while.

Looking at Cassie standing in the doorway wanting to talk sent a shiver of both apprehension and anticipation flowing through Dottie. She gave Cassie her full attention.

This was what she was here for.

"I think talking would be a very good thing." She sent up a prayer that God would lead her in what she should say to anything Cassie chose to share.

Cassie snuggled into the lounger, curling her bare

feet under her before meeting Dottie's gaze.

"My name is Casandra Bateman. I'm nineteen and I don't have anybody."

Dottie straightened in her chair. "Hi, Casandra, it's nice to finally meet you. But you're wrong. You have me."

The tears in Cassie's eyes broke Dottie's heart. *Thank You, my Heavenly Father. Thank You so much.* "I know." Cassie smiled, her lips trembling. "I saw Bob today at the diner. He told me he was thinking about asking someone out and he wanted me to know from him because he didn't want to hurt me, but that I needed to know the truth. I told him it was okay, that I was sorry for what I'd done to him. I guess I've made a fool of myself."

"No, you didn't. I'm sure he was flattered. He really is a nice guy. I'm so glad you decided to share the truth with me. I love you like a little sister, Cassie, and I've been so worried about you. Will you tell me about yourself? About your background?"

She sniffed and wiped a tear off her cheek. She seemed so alone, Dottie couldn't stand it and moved immediately to hug her. Her thin shoulders trembled slightly with unreleased tears. Dottie held her tightly, giving her what comfort she could. After a while, she dried her tears, looked sheepish, and Dottie let her go, moving back to her seat. She was overcome with emotions of her own, so overjoyed that God had given her the gift of knowing this young woman. Of being able to show some of His light in her life.

"Foster kid. That's my background. One home after the other," Cassie said brokenly. Picking at the chair cushion, she gave a nondescript shake of her head. "Once I was in one home for eight months… That's when I had my dog. But foster homes never worked out for me. I spent the last two years at a girls' ranch over in the hill country. It was okay. Anyway, I got to go my own way when I turned eighteen, so I found a job in Austin. Me and another girl from the ranch. I was working two jobs, but I was paying my way and I was happy."

She paused then went on before Dottie could form a response to what she'd learned.

"Me and Angie, we started reading the articles in the paper about Mule Hollow. And I don't know…they got me thinking about all the things I'd never had, you know, a family…something, someone to call my own." She blinked hard and looked out across the yard. "I just started cutting out the articles and thinking about Mule Hollow all the time. I even pasted a picture from a magazine of a small town on my mirror." She looked back at Dottie with a sad half grin. But there was light in her eyes.

Dottie's thought about how much she'd been loved growing up and how easy it had been to take that love and security for granted.

Cassie continued. "Then one day, Angie came home with her boyfriend and told me she was moving out. She felt bad. She knew I couldn't pay my rent living there all by myself. But she couldn't help it, I mean, really, she had a chance to start a life for herself and she was taking it. I couldn't blame her. I woulda done the same thing, only I didn't know how to have a boyfriend. Guys never did much look at me like they did at the other girls. I'm kind of a tomboy-looking girl. Not too much special about me."

Dottie dabbed at her tears, but said nothing, not wanting to stop Cassie's flow of words. Still wanting to tell her how special she was.

"Anyway, I stayed there in the apartment until the manager threatened to evict me. What could I do? I was scared, so I wrote him an 'I owe you' note promising to pay him when I could, then I packed my bag and hit the road. I was terrified. I didn't have anywhere to go, and only a little bit of money…so there I was standing on the corner trying to figure out what to do when I saw this bumper sticker on the back of a car. It said, Successful People Make Life Happen. And that's when

I knew." Her voice cracked with feeling, but she straightened her shoulders. "I knew I was going to make life happen. I wasn't waitin' around for anybody else to tell me what to do. I knew what could happen to me on the street. I'd heard plenty of stories from girls I met in the system. So, I got a map at the store and I found Mule Hollow, wrote down the directions and started walking." She nodded, it was a punctuation to the fact. "I changed my name up because I didn't know if my landlord was going to start looking for me 'cause of the rent I owed him. Soon as I can, I'll save up and send it to him. But I couldn't take the chance of getting thrown back into the system because I owed him money."

"Cassie, I thank God that He led me to you that day." She could hardly get the words past the lump in her throat. The poor girl laughed at that, her eyes bright.

"Me, too. I gotta tell you, though. When I saw that rattletrap of an RV bearing down on me, with all that stuff tied to the top of it, I wasn't too sure if I shouldn't run the other way. Then you climbed out and looked pretty harmless. Figured I could take you if I needed to."

"Oh, did you now?"

"You did look pretty puny. But you're looking better now."

Dottie dried her eyes, things were going to be okay. "Well, thanks. I'm feeling pretty strong. It was just all those days of driving had me hurting pretty badly."

"Yeah." Cassie picked at the chair arm some more.

"I was thinking about that. You said the big guy, I mean, God. You said God was with you when you were trapped and that He never left you."

Dottie prayed God would reach out, using her to touch Cassie. "God was with me the entire time and He's been with you, too, Cassie."

"I know," she said thoughtfully, her eyes pooling. "Miss Adela told me that sometimes bad things happen, but that doesn't mean God doesn't care. That sometimes it takes bad things to make people see Him."

"She's right. It happened to me when I was trapped under my house. I don't know how someone makes it through the hard times without God's comfort and the promise that if we commit our lives to Him we'll spend eternity with Him. That we'll live forever with Him."

"It's nice knowing He's with me," she said. "You know, like that country song that that cute Billy Wayne sings. The one where the little boy is waiting all his life for his sorry father to love him and then the stinkin' dad goes and dies, never having told the kid he loved

239

him." She took a shaky breath. "But in the end, the boy realizes he had a father all along, it was God… Dottie, that's how I am."

"Oh, Cassie," Dottie said earnestly. "God's love is so wonderful. He is always there just waiting for people to realize He loves them. I am so thankful you understand that."

"Yeah, like you said, the God stuff is the good stuff."

Dottie smiled all the way from her toes. "You got it right, kid. The God stuff is the best stuff there is."

CHAPTER TWENTY

Brady watched as the car he'd helped repair a flat tire on pulled back onto the road and resumed its path toward New Mexico.

A family lost on vacation.

He'd cautioned the man to be careful, even pointed them in the right direction and waved to the little girl in the backseat as they left. She was a cute little thing with long dark hair and hazel eyes. And she'd chattered excitedly to him the entire time he'd helped her dad fix the flat.

Dottie would have a child that looked like that. The thought plagued him from the moment he'd seen the child.

He groaned. He needed a vacation himself.

It had been two weeks since he'd moved out of his home and Dottie had moved in. Two weeks knowing she was near but untouchable. Two weeks of sheer torture.

He was cracking. Yep, it was true.

Look at him. Standing out in the middle of nowhere staring after some stranger's car like a fool, thinking about the family he'd determined he'd never have. Thinking selfishly that at this point he didn't care, he loved Dottie Hart and that should be reason enough to forget everything and follow his heart.

But he wasn't wired that way.

In a small town not much bigger than Mule Hollow, a sheriff had been shot yesterday during a routine speeding stop. The cop's wife was three months pregnant with their first child. A child that now would never know its dad.

The fatal tragedy was a timely reminder for him to remain strong.

But even still, he realized that his determination was in serious trouble.

Climbing into his truck and heading back toward town his mind went to thoughts of home.

Because the houses were connected by a long gravel drive through the trees he'd noticed for the past two weeks his old house—no, *their* house—had been brightly lit. He'd heard the laughter drifting from open windows as he'd passed by. He'd wanted to stop and see what was going on. But he hadn't.

The laughter hadn't been there the first couple of days. The house had been quiet, as if they were adjusting, then as if a switch clicked on, the party began. Soon after, the candy started appearing. Some nights the scent of candy carried on the breeze all the way to his cabin.

They were cooking with Dottie.

As the miles to town passed memories assailed him of the fun he'd had doing the very same thing.

More reminders were the fruit of the women's labors on sale at Sam's. The cute little bags were sitting in baskets on the counter. They constantly needed replenishing because the cowboys were eating the candy like crazy. They couldn't get enough of the stuff.

He'd bought a few bags himself, trying to eat away the dark cloud that had taken residence above his Stetson.

He missed Dottie. She, on the other hand, seemed to be thriving.

The ultimate Good Samaritan, she was obviously in her element. He'd thought she might venture out to see him, but evidently she didn't miss him at all. Why should she?

She was busy.

Lacy had taken her to Ranger and she'd bought a

van. She now zipped up and down the roads like a small bus service. She was taking care of everyone.

That was what Dottie did. She took care of people. He hoped she was taking care of herself. He wondered how her hip was holding up.

He wondered, well, he wondered a lot of things. But none of them were helping him get on with his life. It was time to be neighborly.

It was time to be a man and just say Hi.

Who was he kidding? It was just plain time to see Dottie. To look into those hazel eyes of hers and hear her gentle voice.

* * *

Dottie was sitting on the farm implement, her Bible open in her lap when she heard Brady's truck. She'd grown so used to hearing it drive by every evening that it didn't register at first that the vehicle had stopped. Startled, she climbed off her perch and walked to the opening of the barn. She'd been planning to walk down to his place and tell him Cassie's news. And now he was here.

He'd just slammed the truck door when he saw her. She squelched the flare of joy seeing him brought her. It was a lost cause when butterflies returned to dance upon her stomach. She'd missed him so much. She had to stop herself from running to meet him. Even though he looked like a stone carving with his eyebrows cranked together and his lips slashing a firm unforgiving line across his face, he was a wonderful sight to see.

"Hi," she said, feeling awkward, unsure of how to act.

"Hi." He stopped a few feet from her. Glancing up toward the house. Looking uncomfortable himself. "Looks like a busy night."

She nodded, her heart swelling at the news she had to share with him. "Jake's here picking up Cassie and Max. He's taking them into Ranger to go bowling."

"Oh, yeah, what's up with that?"

"Something nice. Do you want to sit down? I'll tell you all about it. I'd planned to give you a call later tonight." After all his help with Cassie, he should be the first to know what had transpired.

"Sure."

She wasn't certain why she led him back to her makeshift bench, but there were a lot of people at the house and they needed privacy to discuss Cassie. At least that was what she told herself.

But it was more than that. She wanted to be alone with Brady. To soak up his company while she had the excuse.

"You found the 'country man's bench,'" he said as she hoisted herself onto her perch.

"Actually, Cassie found it, then I adopted it. I come here in the evenings sometimes." She held up her Bible. "It's a good place for some personal time with God." Brady sat beside her, his shoulder grazed hers and maintained tenuous contact. She had a temptation to lean into that closeness, to soak it up and believe that he, too, felt the connection. "So how've you been?"

How had she been? That wasn't a topic she could talk truthfully about to him. It was best to evade it by telling the exciting news about Cassie.

"Cassie accepted the Lord as her Savior this morning."

"That's great. Wow!" he said slowly, letting it soak in. After a second he nudged her with his shoulder. "God knew exactly what He was doing when He put her in your path that day."

"There's more." She knew she was beaming, unable to deny her excitement as she shared Cassie's entire story with him. He grinned the whole time she talked. When she finished, they both sat in silence staring at each other and out across the pasture, just letting the reality of it set in. Cassie was going to be okay. She might have rocky roads to cross yet, but she had a solid foundation to build a life on.

"You did a good thing, Dottie," Brady said at last, looking at her sidelong. "A wonderful thing."

"I didn't do it, Brady. God did."

"True, but you listened to God's voice and you acted. That's what impressed me about you from the moment you told me you drove out of your way to bring Cassie here."

"I don't always do that. Believe me, I'm no saint." She thought for a moment, overcome by a sudden overwhelming anger. "What about you? Do you listen?"

He shrugged. "Not always. Not like I should."

"You should rethink your choices. I can't believe God wants you living alone." She'd said it all before, but at some point the man had to listen to reason.

"We've been over this," he snapped, pushing from the seat to stand a few feet away from her.

He was angry. But she didn't really care. It was the truth and she couldn't ignore it. She cared for Brady. There was no denying it. No avoiding it. And when you cared about someone, you wanted what was best for them.

Laughter drifted from the house as a door opened, then Jake's truck roared to life. Silently they listened as the sound disappeared down the drive.

"A local sheriff was killed yesterday." The words were harsh as he slammed his Stetson to his head, his eyes unblinking. "He left a wife and unborn child. A child that will never know his father—don't you get that?" His eyes glittered with fury.

That did it! A girl did have a breaking point. Sliding from her perch, she rammed her hand to her hip and glared up at him. "Believe me, I get it! Do I ever get it! My heart breaks for that family, just like yours does. But, Brady, you can't let tragedy define your existence. Where is God's joy in that? Where is the hope that Christ has given us? You live your life like a dead person, hiding behind fear. How does that feel?"

"What?" He took a step back, his jaw slack.

She stepped closer, knowing she was onto something important. "It's easy to tell someone else to trust the Lord. Isn't it, Brady? To admire someone else's faith rather than activating your own."

He dipped his chin and gazed at her from beneath dark eyebrows, his eyes glittering with anger. "What is that supposed to mean?"

"What do you think? When I was lying under all that rubble thinking I was dying, don't you think I had regrets as I replayed my life? My choices? I did. But none of them were because of loving anyone. That was what eased my pain."

"Dottie…" His eyes softened and he took a step closer.

Her mouth went dry, and her anger threatened to dissipate. No! She couldn't cave. This was important.

She struggled to find the words that would reach him. "Brady, you accept risk every day by putting on that badge. Even here, in this small town, you've still committed to accepting the risk. And yet you're not willing to have any personal happiness—"

He rubbed the back of his neck. "Dottie, the risk isn't for me. I'm protecting—"

"Yes—" she gave a humorless laugh "—I know, I know. You're protecting the wife you will *never* have and the children you will *never* know." Crossing her arms, she imagined the steam that should be billowing from her ears.

"Yes, that's exactly who it's about."

"*Argh!* You are the most stubborn man I've ever met! Most people are going to say that loving someone was worth knowing them. Worth the pain of losing them. Love is worth taking a risk for, Brady. And yet, you're the opposite. You won't trust the Lord." She took a deep breath and he stared at her as if she'd lost her marbles.

Maybe she had. She was ranting! She didn't rant. "Look, just like I could never truly know what motivates you, because I wasn't there with you buried

249

alive, you weren't with me watching Darlene struggle to comfort herself and her baby sons after Eddie died. Do you think I wouldn't like to let myself go...to forget everything—"

"You're shortchanging yourself. And God. Not to mention those kids of yours I keep imagining on the playground over there." She waved a hand in the direction of the new playground, and backed toward the barn's exit. He looked confused, glancing toward the end of the barn. When he met her gaze again she felt weak with emotion. "I promised to take the girls to Lacy's. I have to go." Desperate, she spun and hurried away through the barn to the opposite entrance.

Of course, Brady stayed behind. Why would he want to follow a nagging know-it-all?

Outside the door she stopped and glared up at the fading sun. This was ridiculous!

She knew. She had no doubts about what she wanted.

Hadn't she learned that life was a gift? That it wasn't to be wasted. Wasn't that what she'd been trying to tell Brady? A person didn't have to have regrets. A person could take action. Take control. Wasn't that what Cassie had done? That kid had stepped out and chosen against all odds to change her life.

Spinning around, Dottie stomped back through the barn. Back to Brady.

He was standing exactly where she'd left him.

Giving herself no room for chickening out, she marched straight up to him, threw her arms around his neck and planted a kiss smack on his startled lips.

But it wasn't just a kiss. She pulled him close, felt his heart beating rapidly against hers, felt his muscles tremble as he wrapped his arms around her and she laid her love out in that kiss. Felt it flow through her embrace to him. Still, she couldn't let emotion cloud her epiphany. There was a specific purpose to this kiss. It was meant to put a face to the wife he was protecting so gallantly and to make him realize it was *their* children he was refusing to give breath to.

The instant he overcame his surprise and joined the kiss, she backed out of his arms and stalked back the way she'd come. Breathing hard, but determined. It took every ounce of her willpower not to turn around and run back to him on shaking legs. But she couldn't. He had to make the connections from here on out.

"Dottie," he shouted behind her. "Wait! What'd you do that for?"

The man could not be that dense! Turning, she gaped at him, her mouth open in her own surprise, her heart pounding. Did he not get it?

"Oh, please, Brady. Do *not* be a goober." And then she left.

And prayed he could connect the dots and come to his senses.

CHAPTER TWENTY-ONE

"She called me a goober."

"A goober!" Sam hooted with laughter and set a piece of pie in front of Brady. "I'd say she was pert near on the money with that assessment. I ain't one to stick my nose where it ain't got a right to be...but Brady, even an old coot like me can see you have deep feelings for Dottie."

Brady stuck a fork in the cherry pie, not finding anything about this to laugh about. "I could say the same thing to you. Everyone can see you have feelings for Adela."

That stopped Sam's laughter. It dried up like the water of the Red Sea. He looked as if he'd swallowed barbed wire.

It was closing time and the diner was empty. Brady had just made it there as Sam was locking up, and the old man had taken one look at him and offered pie and coffee. Now they were alone.

After a second, he nodded somberly at Brady's assessment. "Yep, ya might say I'm a goober myself."

Pouring himself a cup of coffee, he took a stool beside Brady, suddenly looking older than his sixty-something years.

It was the first time Brady had ever seen Sam sitting. They both stared into their coffee, dazed. Took a sip, then set their cups down with echoing thuds. The clock ticked as they contemplated their goober situation.

Sam glanced at him. "I fell in love with Adela the first time I saw her. Been in love with her ever since."

"When was that?" Brady couldn't help it. He was curious.

"I was ten and she was about seven. My dad had just moved us to Mule Hollow to take ownership of the dry-goods store. Adela came into the store that first day with her mother to purchase supplies for their boardinghouse. Adela looked like a princess in her frilly pink dress. The most beautiful creature God has ever made. Inside and out."

He stopped talking, but he'd hooked Brady. "So what happened?"

"Theo Ledbetter. That's what happened. He was

just as in love with her as I was. Only difference, she loved him back. Theo was the luckiest man on God's green earth." Sam took a swig of coffee and stared hard at Brady. "I know Adela has feelings for me, but I know it ain't the same. The look in her eyes when she speaks his name is enough to make a man jealous of a dead man."

Brady thought about that. "Mr. Theo's been dead, what, fifteen years?"

"Sixteen years, two months."

"So what's keeping you from asking Adela to marry you? I mean, you've been in love with her all these years and it's obvious she has feelings for you."

Sam laughed. It was a harsh laugh. "That right there, son. She has feelings for me. And I ain't got the gumption to see if those feelings are strong enough to say yes if I go and pop the question. She still loves Theo, always will. I can't fill his shoes."

Brady drained his coffee cup with a long gulp and couldn't help thinking about the kind of regret Sam was feeling. He'd spent his life loving a woman, but too afraid to risk rejection by putting words to his feelings. It was a sad state of affairs.

"I'm a goober for sure, son," Sam snapped, gathering up the empty cups and heading to the sink. "You want to tell me why Dottie thinks you're one?"

Brady sighed in exasperation. "Do you ever regret that you never married anyone else?"

"'At thar ain't a real easy question to answer. God didn't never see fit to send me anyone else to love. Only one woman for me."

Yeah, he understood that. Brady stood up. "Thanks for everything, Sam. One goober to another goober, you ought to give Adela a chance. Tell her how you feel."

"You gonna take yer own advice?"

"Sam, I'm going to do something I should have done a long time ago. I'm going to pray about it."

"Giraffe!" Esther Mae squealed.

"Esther," Norma Sue snapped. "Do you see any spots on that drawing? It's a horse, I tell you!"

The small group of women gathered around the drawing board were doubled over laughing at Esther Mae and Norma Sue. On the floor at their feet the toddlers played with an array of toys. Rose, who was responsible for the bad art, stood beside the drawing chuckling and shaking her head, denying that either rambunctious guess was correct. She looked relaxed and happy. Even Stacy was laughing, softly.

"A horse! Norma Sue, have you lost your ever-lovin'

mind? You ever seen a horse with a neck like that?" Esther Mae scowled at Norma, daring her friend to defy her. Suddenly her eyes grew big and she bolted from the couch like a red-topped cannonball. "I got it! It's a, ah—hang on—" She fiercely waved her hands in front of her face like she was combating the attack of the invisible bees. "I know it. It's one of those funny-looking, hairy-horse, half-lama things. An alpacker!" She whooped the word out like she'd just made a slam dunk. "That's it, isn't it, Rose? It's an alpacker."

"Alpaca," Stacy offered timidly from her position deeply ensconced in an armchair by the window.

"Yes!" Rose agreed. "You got it, Stacy."

"Hey, that's what I said," Esther Mae's whine quickly turned into laughter as she looked at Stacy. "But it's the one who pronounces it right that wins. So, that means it's your turn to draw us a picture."

Stacy looked as if she wanted to sink into the cushions and disappear, but Esther Mae wouldn't have it. "There you go, sweetie, don't be afraid." She reached a hand down and pulled Stacy up. "Remember, you're among friends."

From where she stood leaning against the doorframe Dottie's heart swelled as Stacy moved pensively toward the drawing board. Rose handed her the marker and patted her shoulder.

"It's fun, Stacy. And you can draw far better than me."

Though Dottie didn't feel like joining in the fun, she was enjoying watching the bonding between her friends. She was reminded of that first morning in Mule Hollow when she realized what a utopia the little town was and how healing it could be for hurting souls. God had known all of this.

Tonight was a practice run for Stacy and the others. Adela, Molly Popp and the other boarders were hosting a welcome party at Adela's in three days for the new Mule Hollow residents. It had been decided that a gathering with Lacy, Esther Mae and Norma Sue would help prepare them for a larger crowd. That group would prepare them for anything! Dottie smiled, realizing the wisdom in the decision. It was another slow step toward healing their wounded spirits.

The buzzer sounded and Dottie went to retrieve her hot chocolate from the microwave. As much as she was thrilled about everything transpiring in the next room, her heart was heavy with thoughts of Brady. It was still hard to believe what she'd done. She'd kissed him! On purpose!

A lot of good it had done her.

She was settling into a chair at the table when Lacy swept into the room, a vibrant swirl of color.

"Hey, what's up, Dottie? I just got baby Bryce to sleep. He's so sweet." She grabbed a bottle of water out of the refrigerator and nodded toward the living room when a burst of laughter exploded. "Sounds like they're having a blast in the next room. Just what the doctor ordered."

"Oh, yeah, they're bonding like bees and honey."

Lacy pulled out a chair, swung her leg over the top of it and sat down with a thud. "How about you? You've been very quiet since y'all arrived. What's going on? Or do you not want to talk about it?"

Dottie took a deep breath, she really did need to talk to someone. "Have you ever done something and then wanted to whack yourself?"

Lacy choked on her water. "You're asking *me* that question!" she exclaimed after overcoming her coughing fit. "Me, who always needs at least a couple of good whacks before breakfast. Haven't you heard? I'm the queen of sticking my foot in my mouth. Or acting before I think about what I'm doing. Just ask poor Clint. That man has to love me bunches and bunches to put up with my shenanigans. This is about Brady, isn't it?"

Dottie nodded.

"Does he know you love him?"

It was Dottie's turn to choke. Lacy started slapping

her on the back as she wheezed and tried to gain her breath back. "How—"

"Did I know?" Lacy almost fell out of her chair she laughed so hard. "Dottie, everyone knows. We've just been waiting to see when the two of you would figure it out. For a few days there we weren't certain what the Lord was doing when we thought you were leaving town and all. Norma Sue was ready to hog-tie the both of you in the same room until you came to your senses. But then you told us the shelter needed to relocate and we were all ashamed because we had doubted the Lord. Imagine that, God has things under control without the matchmakers of Mule Hollow's input!"

Dottie drew a slow circle on the table with her finger and tried to grasp a firmer understanding of what Lacy was saying. How did everyone know something that even she hadn't known until recently? She blinked. She loved Brady, but it was yet to be seen if he loved her. "Don't tell me you didn't know?" Lacy gasped, snapping her orange fingernails on the table. "Girl, that man hasn't looked at anyone the way he looks at you. Believe me, we've been on the lookout for sparks."

Dottie didn't know how much she could tell Lacy, but she really needed someone to talk to. The laughter coming from the living room told her that the fun was still keeping everyone else busy. So she took a deep breath and lifted her eyes to meet Lacy's. "I do love him, Lacy. And I didn't want to stay here because I didn't think I could live every day seeing him and knowing that I couldn't have him."

"Why can't you have him? I don't get that at all. Go for it."

Dottie didn't feel she had the right to discuss Brady's reasons for his choices. "It's not that easy. Let's just say that he has reasons that are strong enough to make him have convictions that I might not be able to overcome. And in a way I understand. But when I tried to talk to him earlier, I couldn't help preaching. And then I kissed him."

"You kissed him! Now, *that's* what I'm talking about."

Dottie grimaced, still not comfortable with it. "I don't know. I called him a goober when he asked me what the kiss was for."

Lacy slapped the table, chuckling. "Yep, call it like you see it. He is acting like a nut."

Dottie shook her head. "He really has strong reasons for why he won't marry. He thinks he's protecting the family he'll never have because of his convictions."

She'd said it. She'd given away part of his confidence. "I...I shouldn't have told you that. I'm sorry, Lacy, he hasn't shared that with anyone except me."

"It's okay. My lips are sealed. But the fact that he shared it with you speaks volumes. Don't you agree? So, are you going to sit back and do nothing? Brady needs you. He really does."

Dottie couldn't answer. She'd tried the kiss and had gotten shot down. The man hadn't even understood what it was meant for!

How could that be?

"Dottie, listen to me…after all you've been through I look at you and see a woman who walks with God. You inspire me. Like me you came to Mule Hollow with a mission and you're committed to seeing it through. Don't—*do not*—let this get you down. I know that's easier to say than to do, but have faith. Girl, just look back over what God has done in your life—you *cannot* do that and not believe that it's all taking you somewhere."

Dottie stared at the plucky woman, whose white-blond hair heightened the blue of her eyes. They glowed like topaz, encouraging Dottie with earnest sincerity. As Dottie nodded, Lacy reached for her hand. "Can I pray with you?"

Dottie's spirits lifted. "Yes. I would like that." Closing her eyes, a feeling of peace flowed around her and she realized in that moment that God hadn't just sent her on a mission for Him. He'd sent her to a community of wonderful women who could minister to her needs also. She thought of Adela, and her wise words; she thought of the way Norma Sue and Esther Mae ministered to her in their unique way, and she thought of Lacy. Bold in her love of God, forward in her expressions of God's love and undaunted in her passion to share Him with all who she encountered. As she prayed, Dottie felt better. She'd needed a reminder that she wasn't alone.

* * *

After dropping her passengers off at the house, Dottie drove through the woods to Brady's house only to find that he wasn't there. She had planned to tell him she shouldn't have kissed him. That she'd stepped out of line during their talk. True, she loved him. True, she wanted to find some way of making him see reason. To make him understand that she would rather spend one day as his wife than to never have loved him at all. But throwing herself at him wasn't the way to do it.

During Lacy's prayer she'd realized she hadn't behaved in a manner she was proud of. She'd acted on impulse. And while impulse was a great thing for having fun and…and keeping life interesting, looking back, it wasn't the way she should have approached this situation. Obviously!

But, Brady had bolted. What must he think of her? She'd pretty much humiliated herself. And she couldn't apologize. She couldn't take it back. It had been three days and he was still gone.

Take a deep breath, Dottie.

To top it off she was talking to herself again.

A breath was a good idea. She inhaled slowly. When he hadn't been home, she'd first assumed he'd been called out on a late call. That some emergency had occurred and he was needed. Mule Hollow's hero. Always on the go. That's why he needed someone to show him how special he was. Someone to be there for him. By morning, when he still hadn't come home she'd started worrying. She hadn't slept at all. First she'd sat on the porch waiting. When he hadn't come in by 2:00 a.m., she'd gone inside to her room and lain on the bed listening for the growl of his truck as it passed by. But it had never come. At six, she pulled on a pair of jeans and a shirt, shoved her feet into tennis shoes and jogged to his house. Just in case she'd dozed without realizing it and missed him passing by. But he wasn't there. By noon word had circulated that a deputy from Ranger had arrived to fill in for Brady during his absence.

She couldn't figure it out. He could have told her... but really, what business was it of hers?

Theirs was an odd relationship.

Who was she kidding? They had no relationship. Everyone was astonished that Brady had just left town without letting anyone know. It wasn't like him. He was more responsible than that. He would have at least told Clint where he was going, and if Clint knew what was going on he wasn't saying.

Not that Dottie was asking any questions.

It wasn't as if she had any hold on Brady. Really, the man was simply her landlord. And not much of that. What he was charging the shelter for the use of his home was ridiculously low. The man was sometimes too good for his own good. Of course, that was exactly why she loved him.

Then of course it hit her again. She had no hold on him. She had no reason to worry about him! None. He was a free man with no ties to anyone. Exactly the way he wanted it. He could come and go as he liked. He had it all figured out.

He wouldn't have to worry about anyone missing him while he was alive. Or if he was dead.

Except he was wrong. She worried.

But obviously it didn't matter.

CHAPTER TWENTY-TWO

"Hey, Max, how's everything going?" Dottie forced a smile and a lilt into her voice as the teen came out onto the porch, where she was rocking baby Bryce.

"It's going great. Did I tell you lately that I'm glad we're here?" He grinned big, showing a dimple on the left side of his smile.

Despite her sadness, the happiness on Max's face brought her joy. The spring in his step, compared to the kid who'd slunk off the van that first day, was priceless. "Let's see, I think this is your first time today. So I'd like to hear it again before the night is over."

Max grinned and tweaked Bryce's toe. "Hey, little buddy," he said. The young man was like a big brother to all the younger boys. Sinking into the chair beside her, he played a tune with his hands on the chair arms and looked at her intently.

"You know, Dottie, I'm not kidding about what I say. My mom is happy now—back in California, I didn't care if she was or not. Do you know that Jake told me he didn't have a mom? He was raised by an aunt who coulda cared less if he came or went. He and Cassie, they got to talking about their lives the other night when we went to check on some cows. They were way off in the back pastures of Mr. Clint's ranch, it was cool. Anyway, listening to them talk, I got to thinking about how I didn't have a dad, but I had a mother who loves me a lot. That makes me lucky. So now I want my mom to get lucky and meet a nice cowboy. You know, maybe they could fall in love. Don't you think that'd be a real good thing?"

"Oh, no." Rose came out of the house carrying a bowl of popcorn. "So now you're trying to fix me up and marry me off?"

Max turned red. "Well, Mom, I just thought it'd be cool. I was at Sam's the other day with Jake and Cassie and there were a couple of cowboys having lunch with two of the teachers who live at Miss Adela's. Jake said he thought they were getting serious. That everyone was thinking there was going to be wedding bells ringing again, and well, it got me to thinking."

"Sugar, stop thinking about it, I don't know if I want

to ever marry again. I'm certainly not going out of my way looking for love."

"You don't have to, Mom. Tonight at Miss Adela's there's gonna be a roomful of cowboys. Just make sure you put on some of that nasty lip gloss and comb your hair real good."

Dottie listened quietly as she watched the sleepy expression on Bryce's sweet face. She wanted love. She wanted Brady and she wanted a baby so badly that there was a physical ache inside her heart. It was something she hadn't realized she longed for until she'd met Brady.

She'd been praying hard for the last three days. They had this party to go to at Adela's in just a few hours. It was the last place she wanted to go. She wanted to hide under the covers, but it was a party to introduce Rose, Nive, Lynn and Stacy to everyone. She had to go. It was actually the first gathering of townspeople only. And despite what Rose was saying, there would be plenty of wonderful wranglers there just itching to talk to her.

Which was the plan.

Max was right. This party wasn't being thrown for everyone just to say hello. Oh, *no,* there was matchmaking in the air. Norma Sue, Esther Mae and Adela would be watching and comparing and looking for sparks. Those three women loved sparks. If there was even the slightest flicker between Rose and a fella, they'd zoom in and the games would begin.

She just hoped there wouldn't be heartache. "Rose, Stacy is a nervous wreck," Dottie said.

"We're really going to have to stay close." That was her mission tonight. This wasn't about her but her friends.

"You can count on me," Rose said, smiling. Looking happy.

"Emmitt has a crush on her," Max quipped, his dimples showing. "I saw him at church Sunday. He never took his eyes off her. He looked all dreamy eyed, and when she glanced over at him and caught him staring he turned about as red as ketchup."

"That's the shy cowboy, right?"

"Yeah, he don't say much. He works for Mr. Clint. I helped him feed last Saturday. He whistles a bunch instead of talking. It's neat. He can whistle whole entire songs."

Dottie remembered the way he'd looked picking up that diaper for Stacy that first day. It just might take a gentle quiet man to heal the wounds inflicted by violent men in Stacy's life.

Stacy came outside carrying a warmed bottle. Silently she took her seat in the swing beside Dottie and took Bryce. He immediately accepted the bottle. Stacy smiled down at him. If she never found love from anyone other than her baby, Stacy was okay. She seemed content. But Dottie felt as if God hadn't brought them here without reasons. She was looking forward to seeing His plans unfold.

She was just at a loss as to what was happening in her own life. God had her really confused. Then again, as Adela had said, that was God's prerogative. He could do what He wanted to do. What she could do was know that God had a plan for her life. She would trust Him. She would focus on her work, pray for Brady, but let God work things out in His time. In His own way. Not hers.

At least that was her hope. Who knew what she would do next?

Brady pulled into the parking space and stared down the road at Adela's. Tonight was the welcome party for the No Place Like Home ladies.

Taking a deep breath, he opened the door of his truck and stepped to the pavement. This was it. He'd made a mess of things. That was for certain.

Straightening his tie, he rang the doorbell. Cassie opened the door, a scowl on her face when she saw him.

"Oh, it's you."

The kid was mad at him. "Can I come in?"

She shrugged. "Suit yourself. But I ain't guaranteeing you're gonna be welcomed."

She turned, and hair flouncing, stomped away, leaving him standing alone in the open doorway. Why was she mad at him?

He removed his hat and stepped inside, running a hesitant hand over his hair. The rooms at Adela's were filled to capacity and reeked of cologne and boot polish. He'd never seen so many spiffed-up cowboys in his life. He'd always felt as if he was stepping back in time when he entered Adela's huge home, but tonight, with all the slicked-down hair, scrubbed shiny faces, jeans and cowboy boots, it really looked like the clock had turned back to the Wild West days and the cowhands had come a courtin'.

Mule Hollow was looking up.

She saw him first. As he scanned the room, he found her standing across the crowd still as a statue, watching him. Her hair, dark as night, was swept up in a soft bun thing on her head; wispy strands framed her delicate features. It made her look more elegant than ever. Looking at her, he couldn't help remembering the way she'd kissed him. Right there in the barn out of the blue. He wondered if she knew what that kiss had done?

He took a deep breath. It had been a long three days.

Three intense eye-opening days.

She was about to find out exactly what she'd done.

Dottie couldn't believe she was looking at Brady. He was back, standing there across the room taller than any man in the room and looking better than a man had any right to look. She'd sensed him before she saw him. As if her heart knew the moment he stepped into the room. But her heart faltered as she studied him. He looked different.

Something had changed.

And her heart told her it wasn't in her favor. It was the look in his eyes that told her. There was that same flare of awareness in them that she'd come to realize was only for her. And yet there was something else.

And that something scared her.

She knew before he started toward her that she'd lost him. Maybe it was the way his shoulders slumped as he moved through the living room, as one after another person in the room stopped talking and parted to let him make his way to her. Maybe it was the way his beautiful dark eyes glittered hard, as if he was about to do something he didn't really want to do. But that was probably wishful thinking on her part.

She wasn't the only one who saw it. The room that had been awash in conversation had become as silent as the church during a funeral.

He wore a tie. *Like he was going to a funeral.* All eyes were on her. Suddenly she couldn't take it. He was almost to her and she looked around for escape.

She couldn't have him breaking her heart right here in front of everyone. Whirling away, she slipped through the doorway and into the kitchen. She almost slammed into Norma Sue and a large bowl of red punch.

"Whoa there, Dottie! You look like you've got a pack of wild dogs chasing you."

Dottie searched the room, not certain why she was running and not knowing where she was going. All she knew was Brady had been gone all this time, and now, here he was and she was nervous. Mad. Happy. All at the same time.

"Dottie," Brady said, entering the kitchen, taking it over with his presence.

"Brady!" Norma exclaimed, saving Dottie from saying anything right away. "Well, boy, it's about time you showed your face again. When you going to get right the Lord's plan and ask this wonderful woman to marry you?"

So much for beating around the bush. Dottie

almost laughed at the way Norma was glaring at him. He glared right back at her, jerked his head in the direction of the party.

"Don't you have somewhere to be?"

Norma Sue frowned. "Who, me?"

"Norma," Brady scowled.

She let out an exaggerated huff of air. "Well, I reckon I can take this punch in there to that thirsty mob, so long as you make good use of the privacy I'm affording you."

Dottie watched her leave, then she turned and headed for the back door. She could see all the faces staring toward them from the other room. She didn't want an audience. Humiliation shouldn't be public.

"Dottie, would you wait?"

His voice was gentle behind her and that was all it took for the butterflies to start dancing. Closing her eyes, Dottie leaned her forehead against the doorjamb and prayed that the Lord would give her strength. She'd been praying for days.

"Where have you been, Brady?" she asked. Determined not to pry but so curious she couldn't help asking.

"I went to see Darlene and the boys."

Dottie should have known he would go to see his partner's family. It would be in his character to keep in touch with them. Suddenly, she felt jealous.

And she hated herself for it.

Turning, she leaned against the doorframe. Her hands tucked behind her back to keep them from trembling. "How are they?" She might be jealous, but she was interested in their well-being.

He nodded. "They're actually doing well. Darlene's happy. She just remarried."

Dottie closed her eyes, relief sweeping through her. Relief and joy for Darlene. At least she was moving on. "Dottie, I know life moves on. That life doesn't come to a standstill when someone dies. I realized, watching the twins with their new dad, that God's given them a fine man to raise them. Eddie would be pleased."

Dottie watched the emotions on his face. The regret for Eddie not seeing his children grow, but the acceptance that they were in good hands. She took a shuddering breath and bit her lip to keep it from trembling. A tiny flame of hope began to build inside her heart. He took a step toward her, his expression pensive, nervous. With his hair slicked down and his tie on, it struck her that maybe it wasn't a funeral he was going to—he looked like a cowboy going courting on a Saturday night!

Oh, my goodness. Could it be?

"Dottie, I know I've been saying some pretty strong

things. And I know I haven't given us too much of a chance. And I know this may be coming out of left field all sudden like." He dropped to his knee and Dottie jerked to attention.

"Brady!" she gasped as he took her hand.

"I love you, Dottie. I've loved you from the moment we were walking down Main Street that first night and you looked up toward heaven and winked at God. He knew you had a way of looking at life that I needed. I know I've been a goober, as you so eloquently put it. But I know now that you were right…and if you would be willing to take a chance on one hour with me or fifty years, whatever time God gives us, I would be honored if you would marry me." His voice trembled with raw emotion.

"Oh, Brady." Dottie cupped his face between her hands. "I—"

"Just say yes!" Esther Mae yelped.

Dottie glanced toward the doorway. She'd forgotten all about it! Now, it was crammed full, from top to bottom, with faces.

"Ow!" Esther Mae shrieked from about midway down the pileup, having been elbowed by Norma Sue, who was squeezed in just beneath her in the stack.

"Hush up, Esther Mae. You might break the moment."

"The moment! Norma Sue, I swannee you'd think I didn't have a brain in my head. Look at them. They're perfect for each other and he's down on his knees, for cryin' out loud!"

Dottie looked back at Brady and he winked. "Yes." It was all she could do to get past the lump of tears clogging her throat.

Brady swept her into his arms and kissed her before the word completely left her lips.

She heard the cheers. She heard the laughter, but all of it faded to the background as Brady's lips met hers. "No regrets," she whispered when he gave her room to catch her breath.

"Never."

"So," Cassie said, emerging from the crowd and flinging her arms around them. "Do I get to be the maid of honor? You know, I always did want to get to do that."

Dottie laughed, looking from Brady's shining eyes to Cassie's. What a wonderful web God did weave when He put the kid in her pathway.

"The position was meant for you."

Cassie's smile could have provided energy for Mule Hollow for the next ten years.

"Good, then you can be mine."

"What!" Dottie and Brady gasped at the same time

and Cassie smirked.

"Hold on to your bootstraps. I told Jake I needed a little time to grow up first."

Dottie laughed and she and Brady reached around the kid to embrace her.

Dottie kissed her forehead. "It sounds like you already have, kiddo."

"Thanks to the two of you." She kissed Dottie's cheek then Brady's. "I love you two."

And then she slipped from between them, and Brady easily pulled Dottie close again.

"So, Dottie Hart. Tell me about these kids you keep talking about on that playground out behind the house."

Dottie touched his dear face and her heart swelled with the goodness of God's plan for her life.

"Oh, Brady," she sighed against his lips. "You are going to love them so much."

He smiled, leaning back to study her face. "I'm planning on doing just that." He dragged a finger down her cheek and lifted her chin so he could look fully into her eyes. "But first, I'm going to love their mother with all my heart."

Why I chose to set the *Texas Matchmakers* series in the Texas Hill Country

I'm a central Texas gal, living in pure cowboy country between Dallas and Houston. But for *The Texas Matchmakers* series I needed an area that was more remote. After all, for these stories to work I needed the cowboys to have to travel over an hour to get to the nearest larger town. Cowboy's work most days from daybreak to dark, making socializing any distance away from the ranch hard to do. Therefore, I chose the beautiful, varied terrain of the far, outer edges of Hill Country where towns are spread out and ranch land is vast.

The hill country is also known for its massive blankets of Bluebonnets in the spring, its gorgeous sunsets and rocky rolling hills that enable visibility to go for miles….which worked perfectly for my series. There are also rivers and cool springs and creeks that weave through the terrain making perfect places to add a little romance to my books. But also, the dangers of flash flooding is always there, adding danger to the stories when I need it. For the setting of a book, the hill country is perfect.

If you ever visit my home state and are looking for an area made for a wonderful road trips—which I love! One of my favorite places and a must see is the Enchanted Rock. This granite dome is one of the largest in the United States. It's also one of my dad's favorite places which makes it even more special to me. I hope you enjoy the few photos of the area that I've chosen to share—there were just too many to choose from!

So there you have it, why I chose to place my series in this area. I hope you enjoy my vision of the area surrounding my tiny fictional town of Mule Hollow.

Interview with Debra Clopton on Writing Romance

1 – Did you always know you wanted to write romance novels?

No, it never crossed my mind that writing was a possibility! Not until the end of my senior year of high school when my English teacher, who loved my writing assignments, suggested I should be a writer. I loved to read romance, and was drawn to cute romantic movies—Doris Day, Audrey Hepburn-but *me* writing a book never crossed my mind. But once that seed was planted I knew writing romance was what I wanted to do.

2 – As a romance writer what are your greatest goals?

To write books that touch reader's hearts and help them smile. Writing romance, *Dream With Me, Cowboy* to be exact, helped me smile again during the darkest days of my life, after my first husband's sudden death. Immersing myself into a story gave me an escape that I needed at that time. My greatest joy is when a reader writes and lets me know that my little books helped them smile when they needed it most.

3 – *What was your motivation for this Texas Matchmakers series?*

I love fish out of water stories, spunky heroines out of their element, shaken up by amazing cowboy heroes— those inspire me and I wanted to have a place to explore those storylines. Also, I knew when I began plotting this series I wanted to show my love of small-town living. I wanted to give readers a new setting full of a loveable cast of friends to read about. And I had such fun creating this world.

4 – *Where does your inspiration usually come from?*

From everything! Movies, conversation, true stories I hear or read that intrigue me and make me wonder how it would feel to be in that persons shoes…that really draws me in. Triggers for my imagination are everywhere—character's pop into my head right in the midst of a conversation with someone or the first line of a story will come to me and intrigue me and I MUST find out what happens after that line. If I want to know then I assume my readers will want to know too. Life inspires me. People inspire me. God just created me to do this and inspiration is everywhere.

5 – What's your secret to creating a compelling romance?

I strive to entertain my readers through the entire story—I love to try and keep my readers awake at night! I create a strong connection between my hero and heroine and amp up the tension as I go. There must be laughter and issues of the heart mixed together—I love setting up the cute meet of a story putting the hero and heroine at odds and then throwing them together in a fun, entertaining way to draw the reader into the story. Conflict of the heart and exterior world must wrap together so that the reader is rooting for that first kiss and the resolutions they arrive at as they work together to solve the deeper issues and fall in love along the way.

6 – What is the most valuable advice on writing you ever received?

Write the next book! And that's what I'm always doing. Not just because readers want the next book but because I want to see where the series is going. I LOVE the process of a new blank page...the possibilities are endless and I cannot wait to discover what is waiting for me to type onto that page. Of course I love getting to The End too. You know...I just love the whole process.

7 – Where can we find out more about you Debra Clopton?

On my website: www.debraclopton.com, on Twitter and Facebook. You can also join my reader group on Facebook: Debra Clopton's Book Posse. I love to connect with readers wherever you may find me!

More Books by Debra Clopton

Star Gazer Inn of Corpus Christi Bay
What New Beginnings are Made of (Book 1)
What Dreams are Made of (Book 2)
What Hopes are Made of (Book 3)

Sunset Bay Romance
Longing for Forever (Book 1)
Longing for a Hero (Book 2)
Longing for Love (Book 3)
Longing for Ever-After (Book 4)
Longing for You (Book 5)
Longing for Us (Book 6)

New Horizon Ranch Series
Her Texas Cowboy: Cliff (Book 1)
Rescued by Her Cowboy: Rafe (Book 2)
Protected by Her Cowboy: Chase (Book 3)
Loving Her Best Friend Cowboy: Ty (Book 4)
Family for a Cowboy: Dalton (Book 5)
The Mission of Her Cowboy: Treb (Book 6)
Maddie's Secret Baby: New Horizon Ranch Short Story (Book 7)
This Cowgirl Loves This Cowboy: Austin (Book 8)

Cowboys of Ransom Creek
Her Cowboy Hero (Book 1)
The Cowboy's Bride for Hire (Book 2)
Cooper: Charmed by the Cowboy (Book 3)
Shane: The Cowboy's Junk-Store Princess (Book 4)
Vance: Her Second-Chance Cowboy (Book 5)
Drake: The Cowboy and Maisy Love (Book 6)
Brice: Not Quite Looking for a Family (Book 7)

Texas Brides & Bachelors
Heart of a Cowboy (Book 1)
Trust of a Cowboy (Book 2)
True Love of a Cowboy (Book 3)

Turner Creek Ranch Series
Treasure Me, Cowboy (Book 1)
Rescue Me, Cowboy (Book 2)
Complete Me, Cowboy (Book 3)
Sweet Talk Me, Cowboy (Book 4)

Texas Matchmaker Series
Dream With Me, Cowboy (Book 1)
Be My Love, Cowboy (Book 2)
This Heart's Yours, Cowboy (Book 3)
Hold Me, Cowboy (Book 4)
Be Mine, Cowboy (Book 5)
Operation: Married by Christmas (Book 6)
Cherish Me, Cowboy (Book 7)
Surprise Me, Cowboy (Book 8)
Serenade Me, Cowboy (Book 9)
Return To Me, Cowboy (Book 10)
Love Me, Cowboy (Book 11)
Ride With Me, Cowboy (Book 12)
Dance With Me, Cowboy (Book 13)

Windswept Bay Inn
From This Moment On (Book 1)
Somewhere With You (Book 2)
With This Kiss (Book 3)
Forever and For Always (Book 4)
Holding Out For Love (Book 5)
With This Ring (Book 6)
With This Promise (Book 7)
With This Pledge (Book 8)
With This Wish (Book 9)
With This Forever (Book 10)
With This Vow (Book 11)

About the Author

Bestselling author Debra Clopton has sold over 2.5 million books. Her book OPERATION: MARRIED BY CHRISTMAS has been optioned for an ABC Family Movie. Debra is known for her contemporary, western romances, Texas cowboys and feisty heroines. Sweet romance and humor are always intertwined to make readers smile. A sixth generation Texan she lives with her husband on a ranch deep in the heart of Texas. She loves being contacted by readers.

Visit Debra's website at www.debraclopton.com

Sign up for Debra's newsletter at www.debraclopton.com/contest/

Check out her Facebook at www.facebook.com/debra.clopton.5

Follow her on Twitter at @debraclopton

Contact her at debraclopton@ymail.com

If you enjoyed reading *This Heart's Yours, Cowboy* I would appreciate it if you would help others enjoy this book, too.

Recommend it. Please help other readers find this book by recommending it to friends, reader's groups and discussion boards.

Review it. Please tell other readers why you liked this book by reviewing it on the retail site you purchased it from or Goodreads. If you do write a review, please send an email to debraclopton@ymail.com so I can thank you with a personal email. Or visit me at: www.debraclopton.com.

Made in the USA
Coppell, TX
15 August 2020